Praise for *The Mira___ _____ ___arus*

"Readers of The Miracle of Saint Lazarus: A Mystery Twenty Year in the Making *will enter, by the hand of Cuban American writer Uva de Aragón, into a world of police and literary mysteries. The paths of her detective Maria Duquesne and my character Mario Conde will intersect in an amusing fictional game that builds one more bridge between two shores of Cuban culture."*

—Leonardo Padura, Cuban author of *Grab a Snake by the Tail* and *The Man Who Loved Dogs*

"A dead man. A missing baby. A few shadowy characters. And a mother who has never stopped looking for her daughter. With these elements, Uva de Aragón builds a fast-faced novel that has a strong sense of place (you'll feel you are in Miami, drinking Cuban coffee) and nuanced, sympathetic characters. Plus, a healthy serving of Cuban food. When detective Maria Duquesne is assigned a cold case, she chooses a young assistant, Ivan Fernandez, to help her with the investigation. Its twists and turns take them back to the Mariel Boatlift days, with a hop to today's New York. This is a solid mystery with an impeccable ending that will hook you from the first line."

—Teresa Dovalpage, professor of Spanish and ESL, New Mexico Junior College, novelist, and author of, among others, the detective novel *Death Comes in through the Kitchen*

"While trying to unravel a murder mystery and the inexplicable disappearance of a baby girl, Maria Duquesne, a second-generation Cuban detective, does more than solve a cold case. Her detective work compels her to examine her own life and identity, as well as recognize the power of witness testimony. The investigation also reveals how people intent on retaining control over their own lives were compelled to uproot and start again in a new land replete with different practices, customs, language, and values, and it shows how essential it is for exiles, refugees, and immigrants to communicate to subsequent generations their first-hand experiences of totalitarian repression. Impressively translated into English by Kathleen Bulger-Barnett and Jeffrey C. Barnett, Uva de Aragón's novel is a timely meditation on otherness and empathy."

—Asher Z. Milbauer, professor in the Department of English and director of The Exile Studies Certificate Program, Florida International University

"Uva de Aragón debuts in the genre of detective novels with Maria Duquesne, a rich, colorful character which will surely become legendary in the history of Cuban American literature. Duquesne, although universal, maintains her cubanidad with her love for expresso coffee, a great sense of humor, and her deep family values. The Miracle of Saint Lazarus is an excellent mystery novel with all the traditional elements of the genre, plus the originality of delving into the life of the city of Miami with its kaleidoscope of nationalities."

—Marlene Moleón, publisher and editor, Eriginal Books

THE
MIRACLE
OF
SAINT
LAZARUS

THE MIRACLE OF SAINT LAZARUS

A MYSTERY TWENTY YEARS IN THE MAKING

Uva de Aragón

Translated by
Kathleen D. Bulger-Barnett and Jeffrey C. Barnett

BOOKS & BOOKS
PRESS

Starkey Ranch

Published by Books&Books Press, an imprint of Mango Publishing Group, a division of Mango Media Inc.

© Uva de Aragón, 2016. El Milagro de San Lázaro: Un misterio de más de veinte años. Eriginal Books.
© Uva de Aragón, Jeffrey C. Barnett, Kathleen D. Bulger-Barnett, 2018.
The Miracle of Saint Lazarus: A Mystery Twenty Years in the Making.
By Uva de Aragón. Trans. by Kathleen Bulger-Barnett and Jeffrey C. Barnett.
Author photo credit: Wenceslao Cruz

Cover Design: Jayoung Hong
Cover Photo/illustration: Filipchuk Oleg/Shutterstock
Layout & Design: Jayoung Hong

For permission requests, please contact the publisher at:
Mango Publishing Group
2850 S Douglas Road, 2nd Floor
Coral Gables, FL 33134 USA
info@mango.bz

For special orders, quantity sales, course adoptions and corporate sales, please email the publisher at sales@mango.bz. For trade and wholesale sales, please contact Ingram Publisher Services at customer.service@ingramcontent.com or +1.800.509.4887.

The Miracle of Saint Lazarus: A Mystery Twenty Years in the Making

Library of Congress Cataloging-in-Publication number: 2019944229
ISBN: (p) 978-1-64250-124-7 (e) 978-1-64250-125-4
BISAC category code FICTION / Mystery & Detective / Women Sleuths

Printed in the United States of America

To Mario Conde, for inspiring me

Chapter 1

Day 1—Monday, November 2, 2015

When she arrived at police headquarters, Maria immediately noticed that something strange was in the air. She had a sixth sense about these things. Even though everything seemed normal, a thick cloud hung over her colleagues who were glued to their monitors. The hellos were scarce; she knew she wasn't mistaken.

"Any fresh meat?"

For years she hadn't had any other choice but to adapt to the police jargon. At first, it made her sick to her stomach to refer to a homicide victim, a person who had just died, as "fresh meat," but after so many years, it had become perfectly natural.

The only response she got was a few negative shakes from some heads. *What will be, will be*, she thought. Indeed, it didn't take long. As soon as she put up her purse and even before she had sat down at her desk, she heard:

"Mariita, my office, now."

It was the thundering voice of her boss. He had been her father's subordinate for years, and she had known him since she was a little girl.

It had always annoyed her when he called her by the diminutive "Mariita"—typically reserved for relatives and childhood friends—and not the more formal "Maria," if nothing else to maintain the appearance of a professional relationship, which in fact they had despite the sentimental ties.

The chief seemed upset. That became clear when she noticed the evidence that he had stuffed himself with meat pies from the corner bakery, disregarding his persistent efforts not to put on weight and to keep himself fit.

"Have a seat, young lady."

The familial tone put on her guard. *This one wants a favor*, she thought.

"Look, I'm sorry for what I'm about to ask, but I don't have anyone else to turn to. Captain Rios has presented us with a list of unsolved cases in Miami-Dade County that they want to reopen for some reason or another. Rather than reassigning them to the original detectives, he wants other people to work on them so they can offer a fresh perspective. For the moment, he's given us two cases. I don't know if there's a link between them. I've put all the files they brought us in the conference room. I want you to be in charge. Choose whoever you want to help you and, once you see what's involved, let me know what else you're going to need. You know our budget's tight, but I want us to solve this as quickly as possible."

Six foot tall and very fair skinned, with red hair with an occasional touch of gray and eyes as blue as beads, Lawrence Keppler was an American who had gone native, as they say. Not only did he speak Spanish perfectly and loved eating Cuban food and playing dominos, but he even talked with his hands like Cubans, and he spoke so passionately about the Castros that one would think they had confiscated ten factories from him or executed his best friends. The reality was that he had never been to Cuba, but having been born and raised in Miami and having been married for over twenty years to a Cuban had an inescapable effect on him.

Fifteen years earlier, Maria's father had retired, and Keppler would probably do the same before long. He always referred to *Don* Patricio as his mentor and even went to see him occasionally to ask for advice when he had a difficult case, perhaps because he really needed help from a former detective or maybe just so her father would feel useful. She thought it was cute that he included the courteous title of "*Don.*" Larry, as his friends called him, had learned the expression when he spent a semester studying in Seville perfecting his Spanish, and it was his way of showing respect to his former boss. What was certain was that her father loved it when they asked him for advice.

She had never worked on a "cold case" before, and the thought of sitting there, reading old, yellow files didn't seem very appealing. Nevertheless, Maria hadn't agreed to the assignment out of friendship. Even if he had started out as if he were asking for a "favor," it was a direct order.

She understood what the long faces of her colleagues meant that morning. Everyone was afraid they'd get assigned to one of the cases. Once in the conference room, she nearly lost it. Seeing the dates when the crimes had taken place, she was dumbfounded. She took a deep breath, but she had to start somewhere. She opened the first box. She only found some plastic bags and a thin file. It didn't deal with a homicide but an accident. On September 19, 1992, a car driven by thirty-one-year-old Raimundo Alberto Lazo had fallen into a canal on 8th Street at 177th Avenue, near Krome Avenue, and its occupant had died. The file included photographs of the car removal and of the cadaver. She also found a death certificate and a coroner's report that determined the death to be an accident. The plastic bags contained the clothing and shoes worn by the deceased as well as a few personal effects that for some reason hadn't been returned or claimed by the family. For the moment, nothing seemed out of the ordinary except that there was very little information and that the case had been closed hastily. Then she reread the date and understood why.

The accident had taken place only a few weeks after Hurricane Andrew. The police were having a hard time coping. Many officers had lost their homes, but even then the majority were working sixteen and eighteen hour shifts in an effort to help the victims, prevent looting and vandalism, direct traffic, and impose a seven o'clock curfew. There were areas without electricity for more than a month. Similar accidents with people trapped in their cars submerged in canals were frequent in Miami, so it didn't surprise her that they hadn't pursued the investigation further in a such a moment.

She was about to close the file when something caught her eye. Although the old Polaroid was blurry, you could clearly see a child's car seat in the back. She kept on reading until she found what she was looking for. a five-week-old baby had also been in the car, but they had never found the body.

She went out to get a bottle of water before deciding to open the second box of files. All of sudden she got that feeling in the pit of her stomach that comes from a new case, when you realize you're tackling a puzzle; a reality that had been dashed in an instant, and now it was up to her to find the cause and how it had happened.

She was just about to head back to the conference room when her cell phone rang.

It was her father.

"So whatcha doing, *mija*?"

"Just here *playing on the seesaw*, Papi."

Her father chuckled as he always did when she used some old Cuban saying.

"So, you're taking it easy… No new case?"

"No…"

"If you're just goofing off, you could go to lunch with your old man."

"Well, I wouldn't exactly say I'm goofing off. I'm looking over some unsolved cases they want to reopen. Besides, I'm on a diet and I'd prefer to get a yogurt."

"Anything interesting?"

"Yeah, I'm thinking strawberry."

"No, come on, I mean, is the case interesting?"

"I don't know, Papi, I just started looking over the documents. Let's talk later. Behave yourself."

"What choice do I have?"

She headed back into the conference room and opened the second box. She found a bag with the car seat, the birth certificate, a couple of photos of the newborn, and documentation about the search for the body, the false alarm when they had found other remains, the order to close the case, and the various attempts by the mother to reopen it, which until now had been unsuccessful. She wondered what must have happened for them to finally reopen it now that twenty-three years had passed. She went over to the computer and searched through the file where she found a short note:

"Mother asserts having seen missing daughter at Heat game."

She also did a Google search on the girl. She found out about the many efforts carried out by Gladys Elena Lazo to find her daughter because she was convinced that she hadn't died in the accident. She had hired private detectives and sought assistance from associations dedicated to searching for missing children. Over the years, they had made three or four sketches of what the child would have looked like at a given time. The last one, made two years ago, showed a young brunette with large eyes and a fixed gaze. Suddenly, that small, missing child took on life. Was it possible that she hadn't died? And if she had survived, where had she been all these years? And how to even go about looking for her?

She grabbed the phone and dialed the most recent number in the file.

"Hello, is Gladys Elena Lazo there?"

"Speaking."

"This is Officer Maria Duquesne. Is there a convenient time when I could come by and see you at your house?"

Chapter 2

Day 1—Monday, November 2, 2015

Even though she hadn't planned to go out for lunch, she immediately agreed to do so given the urgent tone in the voice that was speaking to her:

"We have to see you right away!"

A rolling stone gathers no moss, she told herself as she put her cell phone into her purse, got her keys out, and headed out into the midday sun.

What could possibly be up with these crazy old women who need to see me so urgently and with all this mystery? The crazy old women in fact were Lourdes and Yolanda, her mother's schoolmates from a childhood long ago in Havana.

They were waiting for her at the most obscure table in the restaurant. Rather than one of the places where they typically met, they chose a small, half-empty restaurant in a seedy strip mall in the Sweetwater area. The surprise must have registered on her face because Yolanda quickly blurted out:

"The fact is that Lourdes has to ask you something very privately."

As the waiter got closer, they lowered their voices. They asked for three glasses of Chardonnay. It was as if they were speaking Chinese. They wound up accepting three Presidente beers.

In response to her inquisitive look, Lourdes began to speak slowly, as if pronouncing each syllable required an immense effort.

"I wasn't sure if I should bring it up... I don't think it's anything... I don't know... Probably... It's just that it seems like...and maybe you..."

Maria was about to lose her patience and to tell her to get to the point, but she noticed a hint of pain in the woman's eyes that made her hesitate and try to comprehend what she was saying beyond the actual words, the meaning behind her gestures and the modulation of her voice that was becoming fainter.

"And?" she succinctly asked while raising an eyebrow.

"Lourdes thinks that Ramon is cheating on her," Yolanda blurted out.

Maria had to make an effort to stifle her laughter. She couldn't bring herself to believe that the seventy-year-old man was up for an affair, even though it wasn't out of the question at his age with Viagra. These days, even Vargas Llosa, who was pushing eighty, was making a fool of himself as a dirty old man in all those photos in *Hola* magazine. When the waiter came back with their food, the women hushed their conversation for a moment. Lourdes's breaded cutlet draped over the plate, along with black beans and plantains. Yolanda had asked for *vaca frita*, that typical Cuban flank steak, with the same side dishes except that the plantains were sweet. As for Maria, she had limited herself to a tuna salad.

When they were alone again, she looked at Lourdes.

"Hang on, what makes you think that?" she asked with all seriousness, as if she were investigating one of the cases back at headquarters.

"Look, when he retired a year ago, he was happy enough watching films on Netflix, listening to the news, reading... He even bought a Kindle. You had to light a fire under him just to get him out of his recliner. A few months ago, he started eating lunch every Thursday with some friends..."

"That's true, because Alicia's husband, Oscar, goes too and they get together for lunch in a backroom at Casa Juancho..."

"Yeah, but now they're also meeting at night one or two times a week, and he never tells me anything... It's all a mystery... And he whispers on the phone."

"Have you noticed any unfamiliar number or a text on his cell?" Maria asked, certain that her friend would have already checked it.

"Well, truthfully, no. The texts only come from the grandkids… occasionally from his sister, and no unknown telephone numbers."

"And his emails?"

"No, but he could erase them."

"A woman's perfume, lipstick on his clothes, anything unusual about his underwear, socks inside out?"

"No."

"Because you checked all these things, right?"

"Well, it's just that I…"

"Yeah, that's what any of us would do. Anything else?"

"I don't know, he just doesn't seem to be himself, like he's not here, he's got his mind on something else. I'm sure he's hiding something from me."

"Is it possible that some type of investment went wrong, and he doesn't want to tell you?"

"I don't think so."

"Any health problems?"

"I always go to the doctor with him…a bit of arthritis in his knee, medicine for his blood pressure…normal stuff for his age."

Worrying about her husband's possible infidelity had not made Lourdes lose her appetite. The waiter came and took away the empty plates. Maria had heroically managed to avoid Yolanda's tempting offer to share her sweet plantains. Years ago, she had gone to Weight Watchers to lose some weight, and she remembered the instructor's dramatic assertions about how Cuban food makes you gain weight. However, she couldn't turn down the croquettes that came with her tuna salad.

They were already having their coffee when Maria asked:

"And so what do you want me to do?"

"I thought that maybe you could follow him."

"Are you crazy?"

"I could pay you."

"You're stark raving mad! In the first place, he knows me…
And besides…"

"He hasn't seen you that much lately, and you're an artist when it comes to disguises with all those wigs and other things you have…and you can take photos."

She couldn't help but grin. It was true. She had had to resort to altering her appearance many times when she worked undercover. There was even that time she had to pass for a prostitute!

"And you've already followed him once…"

"That was more than twenty years ago when you had a similar fit of jealousy and your poor husband was trying to overthrow Fidel…"

"Well, that was when the Soviet Union had just collapsed, and we all thought that Cuba was going to fall along with it. It just needed a little nudge. This time it's different."

"Look, Lourdes, back then I wasn't on the police force and I was working as a private detective, but now as an officer of Miami-Dade County I can't do those things. It's against the law. I could lose my job."

"No, *mija*, not that…"

"Lourdes, I'm absolutely convinced that these ideas of yours are baseless, but if you are still worried a month from now, I'll put you in touch with a detective friend of mine…"

"Geez, I don't know. It's one thing for you to do it, but to employ a complete stranger. I'll think about it. Thanks, Mariita. And please, don't say a word about this to your father."

She was happy to have gotten out of Lourdes's absurd request, and it was true that the police regulations were very clear on the matter. Barring that, she wouldn't have had any recourse but to accept her request. She really did love those two crazy, old women. When they diagnosed her mother with cancer six years ago, they had taken care of everything. They accompanied her to her chemotherapy sessions and brought food to her father. They had acted as nurses, housewives, cooks, psychiatrists, and, when her mother lost her battle and passed away, they adopted her as a daughter and Patrick as a grandson. They even went to his basketball games and yelled more loudly than anyone! When he graduated from high school a year ago and was admitted to the University of Florida in Gainesville, his adopted grandmothers took it upon themselves to buy him everything he needed, from a laptop to a first aid kit.

They said their goodbyes with a kiss, some comforting words, messages for the adopted grandson, and a promise to meet up again soon.

"You're going to see that there's nothing to worry about," Maria told Lourdes to reassure her.

Chapter 3

Day 1—Monday, November 2, 2015

She followed the directions that the GPS gave her and arrived at the humble house in Hialeah without any trouble. She remembered back before the technological advances that help people get around these days, how she would always get lost when she went to "The City of Progress"—a concrete city known for its ubiquitous statues of Saint Lazarus and Saint Barbara in people's yards and its diversity of Cubans from all backgrounds who shared one thing in common: they all clung to the culture of the Island. Even those born in the US like herself—those with college degrees, without a trace of an accent in English, and with a Spanish that left much to be desired—felt Cuban even if they had never set foot on the land of their parents and grandparents. She didn't remember which writer had coined the phrase that being Cuban was an incurable disease, hereditary, and sometimes even contagious, but the author had a point. Her boss, Keppler, was one of the ones who had been contaminated. And she was one of those who had been born with "Cubanness" in her genes.

Maria's heart skipped a beat. The young girl who opened the door was almost identical to the one she had seen in the drawings that showed what the missing baby would look like today. Before she could say anything, the girl said:

"I'm Elena Lozano, Gladys Elena's daughter… Gladys Mercedes's half-sister… You're the detective that called, right? Please come in. My mom will be right here. She was very nervous waiting for you and went to make coffee."

Sure enough, Maria smelled right away the unmistakable aroma of coffee… A much younger woman than she expected entered the room, drying her hands and giving instructions to her daughter. The woman then turned to Maria and said.

"Thank you so much, Detective Duquesne… Come in, please."

She took her to an office with a small desk, a computer, a bookcase, various metal filing cabinets, and a few family photos. Maria didn't have much time to observe her surroundings because the young girl came back right away with two glasses of water and two cups of coffee on a tray.

"Wow, with foam and all. Thank you."

"Sit down, please," said the owner of the house, pointing to one of the two armchairs in front of the desk. She sat in the other.

She's perceptive, Maria thought. *She didn't sit at the desk to avoid creating distance between us.*

"Go ahead, please."

"Would you mind if I take notes and record the conversation?"

"Of course not."

"So, I've been assigned to reopen both of the cases, the accident involving your first husband and also the disappearance of your daughter. I've read what little information there is in the files, which is understandable given that it happened a few weeks after Hurricane Andrew, and I've seen everything on the Internet you've done to try to find your daughter, that you think she's still alive, and that you thought you recognized her recently among the crowd at a Heat game. I want to take the case in a new direction without the influence of the prior investigation. To do so, I need you to be completely honest with me, tell me everything from the beginning, even though you might have already gone over it with other detectives, and that you answer my questions without leaving anything out. Are you willing to do so, even if it opens old wounds?"

"You have my word that I will tell you everything."

"Then let's start at the beginning. Where did you meet Lazo? What did he do? How long were you together for?"

Gladys Elena took a deep breath, as if to gather up the courage before she began to speak.

"Well, Detective, I was born in Pinar del Rio, not even in the city, just in the middle of nowhere. My parents were simple people, good and honorable country folks. If you're Cuban, certainly you know that the worst times of the "Special Period" were in '93 and '94, but even as early as '91 things were already bad. Some of our neighbors began pressuring my father to leave the country with them on a raft. My mother refused to. It frightened her, and she didn't want to risk losing my brother and me. We were just children. My brother was only fifteen and I was seventeen, more or less the same age my children are now. On another occasion, when you have time, I can tell you about the preparations for the voyage and about the journey itself. It was something I'll never forget. It scarred me for life because my father and neighbors died during the passage. Only Raulito and I survived, arriving here without anything and not knowing anyone. Fortunately, at the last minute, the thought of the sea at night terrified my mother, and she refused to get on the raft."

The woman took a moment, perhaps searching for the strength to continue.

"At first, we got help from the government, from the Red Cross. Eventually we found some distant relatives who took us in for a while. My mother suffered so much by herself in Cuba that she braved the journey months later and got here safely. The three of us found work. Things were looking up. The laundromat where I worked—you can't imagine how hot it was in there—is where I met Raimundo, who worked as an electrician. He was much older than me, but we were a lot alike. I had left my boyfriend back in Cuba and, although I'd heard rumors that he was seeing somebody else, I kept receiving letters from him and I still loved him…but the truth is I was falling in love with Ray. I became pregnant and we got married soon after. Our daughter was born prematurely, I don't know why, but thank God she weighed enough and was healthy. I recovered the positive outlook on life I had before the trauma caused by my father's death."

She took a sip of water and continued:

"Then Hurricane Andrew came. We hadn't even been here for a year. Little Gladys was a newborn. She cried constantly. She was colicky. Then we lost power. You wouldn't believe how hard that was with a newborn. Our neighbors, who had a generator, let us keep the baby bottles in their refrigerator. I couldn't nurse her because my milk dried up. It must have been nerves. The heat was unbearable. I don't know how long I went without sleeping. I was exhausted. A few days later, we got a message from my mother that her phone was out but at least she had electricity, and that we should go over there. I didn't have enough energy. That's when the lights came back on. Ray suggested that he take the baby to my mother's so that I could rest. I packed the diaper bag with bottles, formula, diapers, the dirty laundry that needed washed, and whatever clean clothes I had for the baby… Finally, he put her in the car seat and drove off; I laid down and slept for ten hours."

"When did you learn of the accident?"

"Since neither my mother nor I had a phone, she thought that we had a change of plans, and I thought that she had the baby and that Ray was out working. The next morning, a police officer knocked on the door. Someone had seen the car in the canal and when they recovered it they found Ray."

"But not the baby?"

"No…never."

"Do you think that the current could've dragged her off?"

"That's what I thought for a while. It drove me crazy. You have no idea how depressed I became afterwards."

"What made you change your mind?"

"Detective Duquesne, because two years later they found human remains and thought they were hers."

"Yes, I read that."

"Since the police contacted me again, I asked to see the photos of the accident for the first time."

"And?"

"The photos were a bit blurry, but I could see clearly that Gladys's seatbelt was unfastened. All the windows were closed when they took the car out of the water. Only the passenger-side window was cracked open a bit. Where could the baby have gone? And they didn't even find the diaper bag that was placed beside her. Someone took my baby out of the car before it crashed into the canal."

She calmly placed her hand on her chest to emphasize her conviction.

"I know that she's still alive. I know it in my heart."

Chapter 4

Day 2—Tuesday, November 3, 2015

There's nothing like a hot cup of Cuban coffee from any local café to start the day. The coffee she made at home just wasn't the same. Additionally, she liked how the waiters would call her "mi amor" and "mi vida." *And to think that when I was a kid that affectionate treatment annoyed me! You've become soft in your old age*, she said to herself while enjoying the last sip of her strong, sweet coffee.

The night before she had gone to her dad's house for a beer on her way home, had exchanged texts with Patrick who assured her that the semester was off to a good start, and had put together a salad for dinner. She really couldn't put her finger on exactly what it was that worried her, but she couldn't fall asleep. Even when she felt like she was sleeping, she kept thinking about the case.

The previous afternoon, she had finished the conversation in the house in Hialeah when she noticed Gladys Elena looking at her watch constantly. Finally, she said:

"It's just that my husband and son are supposed to get in. Elena understands but they, being men, think that I need to accept what happened and that I'm in denial…"

There were things that now I regret not having asked her, but there will be another time to talk with her.

When she got to her office, the atmosphere was more somber than the day before, but this time she immediately knew the cause. Robert Parker, ex-director of the Miami-Dade County Police, who had been retired for six years, had been found dead in his house at age sixty-two. There was talk of suicide but no one was convinced. There was no rationale for it, and he hadn't left a note. She immediately called her father, who had already heard.

"He was a career man with more than thirty years of service. The first African American to occupy the position. He had a beautiful family. It's impossible that he could've committed suicide."

"Take it easy Papi. I'll keep you updated and come over later, but right now I need to get back to work."

The first thing she did was look for everything she could about Raimundo Alberto Lazo. She didn't find anything: no criminal record, no credit score, no tax returns for the ten years prior to the accident. It took her a couple of hours, but she finally discovered that his social security number really belonged to one Ray Bow who had died in January 1980.

So, Raimundo had stolen the identity of a dead man… Ray Bow. Raimundo Lazo. Without a doubt, it was a false name too. But why? What was he hiding? What was he running from? Who was the man who crashed in the canal in 1992? Was it really an accident or was there another cause of death?

Maria put the files in her briefcase and headed for the morgue. She knew it would be odd not to find Dr. John Erwin there. They knew her well in the building on 10th Avenue, and they let her come and go as she pleased. Early on in her career, she learned the importance of making friends all over the place. She cultivated her contacts. She remembered the names of their family members, from time to time brought them Cuban coffee or a box of donuts, went to all the birthday parties she was invited to, and attended the funerals of their relatives. She attempted to maintain a balance that let her establish a personal relationship without coming off as a suck-up, or, as her dad would say, a "kiss-ass."

She found the old medical examiner performing an autopsy. It had taken Maria a long time to watch this part of the investigative process with ease, but the eight years that she worked in the homicide department had cured her of all apprehensions. She shared some of the details of the case with Dr. Erwin.

The doctor finally finished the autopsy. She kept quiet while he finished writing up the report and giving instructions to his assistants to take the cadaver to the freezer.

"So, Maria, what can I do for you?"

"Well, two things. First I need you to look at this forensic report and tell me if there's any possibility that this man could've been killed instead of dying in an accident."

Erwin took off his gloves, washed his hands, and wiped the sweat from his forehead with a paper towel. He was always sweating despite the cold temperature in the morgue. He was a stocky man with chubby fingers that somehow treated the bodies with astonishing delicacy. He then took the papers that Maria held in her hands and read them for two minutes before declaring:

"Yes…"

"Yes?"

"Yes, it could've been a murder. See, he had water in his lungs which tells us that he was still alive when he crashed into the water. You can only see a small portion of the window open in the photo. It's strange because if he were conscious the logical thing to do would've been to open the window more. Additionally, the autopsy says that he had sustained trauma to the head. They attributed it to the impact of the accident, and that could be, but it also could've been that someone hit him, leaving him unconscious, and then pushed the car into the canal. Now what was your other question?"

"This man wasn't actually who his driver's license or death certificate said he was. What do you think would be the best way to go about identifying him?"

"Certainly you're not thinking about exhuming the body."

"No, not at this time."

"Do you have anything to extract DNA from?"

"The clothing that he was wearing is in a sealed bag."

"Better yet, see if the family kept anything of his, maybe a hair brush."

"It's been twenty-three years."

"You of all people shouldn't be surprised by the things people save from their dead relatives."

She called Gladys Elena to make sure that she would be home and went directly to Hialeah. This time Gladys was alone and she opened the door herself.

"Come in, come in… Excuse me a minute, I was just making coffee," and she ran off into the kitchen.

Unlike the previous visit, Maria took the opportunity to look at family photos. It struck her that the girl that she had met last time, who had a striking similarity to the sketch of the missing baby depicted as young woman now, looked like her father and not Gladys while the boy looked like her and like another young man in one of the photos.

"That's my brother, Raulito," Gladys said when she saw Maria looking at the pictures.

She didn't comment on the similarities. After all, it was very subjective.

"When did you remarry?" she asked in a friendly tone just before sipping her coffee.

"Well, here's how it all happened… Mauricio was the boyfriend that I had left in Cuba, and he came here two years later. Slowly we fell in love again and a year later, in '95, we got married. Little Elena was born on December 19 of '96. It's incredible that she looks just like her sister… I mean, according to the sketch they did of her sister."

When they finished their coffee and sat face to face, Maria turned on the tape recorder, took out her notebook and pen, and began questioning her:

"Where did you, Lazo, and your daughter live before the accident?"

"In Little Havana. Let's see, here's almost all of the information."

She handed Maria a sheet with the address of where they lived in 1992, her mother's address, the address where Lazo worked, names and phone numbers of neighbors and contact lists of their respective coworkers that they were still in touch with.

"You're making my work easy."

"It's taken years…"

"Just two or three more questions… What do you know of your late husband's past?"

"About Ray? Well, very little. He told me that he came on the Mariel Boatlift, that he was from Cardenas, and that he didn't have any family here. But when he died, a long-lost uncle of his showed up and was very generous. He paid all the funeral costs even though the wake just amounted to a few of his friends from work. Ray was a good man. He always told me: *This is the land of second chances and you've been mine.* And he'd also go around saying: *Fidel didn't create the 'new man'; you performed that miracle.*

"Do you know why he said that, if he had been married before, if he had left kids behind in Cuba, if he had enemies…?"

"He talked about a girlfriend that he had in Cuba. He was so overjoyed when the baby came along that I can't imagine that he had any children before. I don't believe he had any enemies either. Why would a poor electrician have any?"

"Your mother didn't live anywhere near the accident. Do you know what your husband was doing in that part of town?"

"I've asked myself that a thousand times and never found an answer. I think that maybe he went to help out one of his friends... In those days, everyone had problems."

"Anything else? Did you save anything of his?"

The lady hesitated:

"If you give it to me, I promise to get it back to you," Maria added.

"Just a minute."

It took her a few minutes to return and she brought out a small suitcase, the kind that no one uses anymore, rectangular, without wheels, and faded black.

"Here are all of his belongings. I have a box with our daughter's things in it as well if you want it, but..."

"Did you ever ask to have your daughter's DNA tested?"

"No, they're too expensive, and they never found her so I didn't think it was necessary."

"True. We can wait. We'll go ahead and test Ray's. One last question. I noticed you never dropped the last name Lazo."

"Well, it's a relatively common name and the baby couldn't know her own name because she was too young, but if she does look for me, it would be easier to find me if I kept the same last name, right? Anyway, Mauricio doesn't ask me about that."

As she was leaving, Maria was somewhat surprised when Gladys Elena gave her a kiss on the cheek very naturally.

"You'll keep me up to date if there are any developments, right?"

"Of course."

When she worked on homicides, the hardest part was always informing the family. The murder of a loved one was the worst thing that anyone could ever endure, or so she thought, but now she wasn't so sure. Living more than twenty years looking for a lost daughter had to be an extremely heavy burden. She had seen it in the eyes of the young woman who still had traces of agony in her gaze.

Chapter 5

Day 2—Tuesday, November 3, 2015

Maria arrived at her home in El Doral eager to cook. That was often the case when she was nervous or worried, but these days—even before Patrick had gone off to college—she seldom ate at home. That's why she had looked for other ways to alleviate her stress, like going to the gym or having a couple glasses of wine. She glanced in the refrigerator and only found a yogurt, skim milk, some whole wheat bread, turkey, cheese, and some vegetables. The choices in the freezer and pantry weren't much better. She was about to give up, but she wound up grabbing her wallet and car keys and headed off to the nearest Publix.

A couple hours later, the aroma of *sofrito* flooded her house. She immediately thought of her mother and smiled, holding back the tears. Even though she knew perfectly well how to make *picadillo*, she searched for the old cookbook by Nitza Villapol. When she opened it, she found a sheet of paper with a recipe for a spinach quiche in her mother's unmistakable handwriting.

She sautéed the onion and pepper in the olive oil, threw in a can of tomato sauce and removed it from the stove. Then, just as she was seasoning the ground beef, an uncontrollable fit of crying overcame her. It happened like that at times, coming in waves, like the ones when she used to go to the beach and the sea was rough, and they made her feel like she was drowning. Maybe that was why she didn't cook that often anymore… The smells unlocked her memories.

She poured herself a glass of Merlot and sat down to relax before finishing the *picadillo*. In recent years, she had thought a lot about her mother's life. As the daughter of a physician-professor and a housewife, Maria Cristina Fernandez Oviedo had belonged to Havana's upper middle class. She had studied at private schools, spent her summers at Varadero, and belonged to one of the most exclusive clubs in the capital.

She was fifteen years old and dreamed of becoming a physician, like her father and grandfather, when Fidel Castro took over and her life changed in an instant.

Less than two years later, her parents decided to get her out of Cuba through the Peter Pan program, by which fourteen thousand Cuban children fled the country between 1960 and 1962. When she arrived in Miami, they sent Maria Cristina to a convent in San Antonio along with other children. The Church's protection didn't last long because shortly thereafter she turned eighteen—the age at which the program ended. The nuns didn't throw her out in the street right away. She lived there a few more months until she put together some savings from her work, and she and some of the other girls who were in the same situation were able to rent an apartment. Since that time—except for a few months after Maria was born and until a few months before her death—Maria's mother had always worked. She never got the chance to study medicine as she had dreamed of doing, but she did complete her nursing degree and became head nurse at the Intensive Care Unit at Baptist Hospital.

Her mother had seldom talked about what she had left behind on the Island. Maria now regretted not having asked her more about her life back in Cuba, especially about her grandfather. Her mother had never gotten the chance to see him again. Two months after she left, he died of a massive heart attack at the age of fifty-seven. Her grandmother joined them by way of one of the Freedom Flights in 1967, when she was only one year old, and since then she had practically raised Maria while her parents studied and worked. When her grandmother passed away in 1987, her mother held her tight and said over and over:

"I'm not going to die yet, I promise… I promise."

She hadn't understood her mother's anguish until now, now that she felt that same sense of desolation, that feeling of being an orphan that came from her absence.

Thank God she still had her father! He had always been her hero, her role model. In recent years, however, she had come to appreciate her mother's inner strength, her quiet demeanor, and at the same time her tenacity to resolve everything, to forge ahead, to keep the family together, and to instill values.

The buzz of her cell phone brought her back to reality. It was a message from her colleague David, telling her that he was close by if she wanted to go out for a drink. Instead, she invited him to come by and share some *picadillo* with her, which he gladly accepted.

She immediately put the ground beef into the skillet along with the raisins, olives, wine, and spices over a low heat. She did the same with the rice once the water had boiled. She set the timer for twenty-five minutes and went to take a shower.

When David rang the doorbell thirty minutes later, the table was set and dinner was on the stove. Dressed very plainly, and with her hair up in a ponytail and just a touch of makeup, Maria didn't look like she was forty-nine. When she glanced at herself in the mirror, right before she opened the door, she thought to herself: *I need to lose ten pounds. This damn curse of Cuban women who have such a big ass!* And she smiled as she thought about her grandmother, a Spaniard, who used that word much more often than her father would have liked.

David and Maria had started their careers at the same time in the Miami-Dade County Police Department. At one time, they had worked together as a team. In other times, like now, they were at separate stations. Both had been married and divorced. David had two sons, more or less the same age as Patrick. In all the ups and downs of their respective lives, their friendship had never wavered one bit. It was easy for them to talk because they had so much in common. Although David's father was American, he felt more kinship with his mother's side and saw himself, like her, as a Cuban American.

"This is the tastiest *picadillo* I've ever eaten in my life. And these plantains!"

"I can't take any credit for the plantains. They're from Goya and come frozen." Maria was pathologically honest.

They chatted for quite some time, she seated on the sofa and David in the armchair. Before long, he got up and sat down beside her. There is something about the body language between a man and a woman that sends a signal. Maria knew that David wanted to make love. She had always denied it, fearing that a romantic relationship might hurt their friendship. He seemed to read her mind:

"The two of us are very alone… We're very much wedded to our work… Nothing is going to alter our friendship."

She felt very vulnerable. She knew that they weren't in love and that it was unwise professionally speaking, but she also knew that David would never hurt her.

When she felt that tingle between her legs that marked the onset of desire, she knew she couldn't resist any longer, and she let herself be gently pushed toward the adjoining bedroom.

Day 3—Wednesday, November 4, 2015

She was happy that David hadn't wanted to sleep over. It was one thing to sleep with a man and another to spend the night with him. She couldn't explain why, but it was different, and she wasn't ready yet for that next step.

She got dressed quickly and made herself a shake with yogurt, strawberries, and protein powder. She stopped along the way to get her coffee and was at the office before nine in the morning.

She began to go over the list of contacts that Gladys Elena had given her and she decided to begin by calling her mother. The phone rang a few times before a woman's voice answered, a voice that seemed to belong to someone younger than she had imagined. Maria identified herself and asked when she might be able to meet with her.

"My daughter told me that I could count on you calling me. Look, I'm driving right now. I still work… It would have to be some evening or on a weekend… Does tomorrow after eight o'clock suit you?"

Maria would have preferred to see her that very day but she jotted down the address and assured her that she would be there the next evening.

It took her longer to find the one who had been Raimundo Lazo's boss, but, once she got a hold of him, he immediately told her that she could see him anytime except between two and four when he took his siesta. She didn't waste a minute and took off to meet with Joaquin del Roble who lived in The Palace, an assisted living community for the elderly. There were several in the city. Don Joaquin—which is how his name appeared on the list that Gladys had given her—lived in The Palace Royale, located on 1135 SW 84th Street, in the Kendall area. It took Maria twenty-five minutes to get there. She found several tall buildings surrounded by immaculately manicured gardens. The clock showed eleven in the morning when she made her way into the lobby. It was quite beautiful and would have seemed like a luxurious hotel if not for the abundance of the elderly. Some were seated and chatting in groups while others were by themselves, reading or simply sitting idly. A few others were coming and going in all different directions of The Palace Royale, which offered them all types of amenities: a hair salon and barbershop, a business center, an art studio, a theater, a bar, and a wonderful dining room that punctually offered them three meals a day. *The ideal way to spend your old age*, Maria thought to herself with a certain skepticism since it all seemed a bit depressing despite being clean and somewhat ostentatious.

Don Joaquin was waiting for her to arrive and came up to her before she had barely gotten in the door. He was a man of small stature and, despite the fragility of his advanced years, one could tell that at one time he had been strong and tough. An abundant head of gray hair crowned his ample forehead. His eyes were bright although they'd lost their sparkle. His thin lips formed a smile when he greeted her:

"Detective Duquesne? Joaquin del Roble, a pleasure to meet you," and he kissed her hand with such elegance that it moved Maria.

"If you'll follow me, I think we'll be more comfortable in the library. Almost no one goes there… People don't read like they used to."

He walked slowly but with a sure step. She quietly followed him, thinking of her father and how she would never want him to live in a place like this, which besides must cost a fortune.

They sat down in two comfortable armchairs and, just as Don Joaquin had predicted, the room was rather empty.

"So tell me, how can I help you?"

"Well, we've recently reopened the case of the accident involving Raimundo Alberto Lazo and his missing daughter, whose body was never found. Her mother believes that she saw her recently and is positive she's still alive. It's my understanding that he used to work for you. I know it was years ago, but anything you could possibly remember, no matter how small the detail, might help me. Look, I've got a picture of him here and another of the two of you together, in case that helps jog your memory."

Don Joaquin took a brief glance at the photos. He shut his eyes, as if he wanted to delve deep into his memory and bring his recollections back to life.

"I remember him vividly, and the accident too. Those are difficult things to forget. Let's see, where to begin…"

"Do you mind if I record our conversation and take notes?"

His blue eyes reflected a deep sadness.

"Go ahead and record. No one cares anymore about the life of an old codger like me, but to tell you about Alberto, I'll have to tell you my story too."

Maria made a note of the fact that Gladys referred to him as Ray, but Don Joaquin knew him as Alberto.

"I hope you have a lot of time because it's a long story."

"I have all the time in the world, and if you get tired I can come back another day."

"So, as you have probably noticed, I'm a Spaniard. Well, an American citizen, but that's just a formality… My father was the mayor of a small town near Zaragoza when the Civil War broke out. I was fourteen, and the war was horrendous. You can't imagine. My father was a prisoner for two years, and, during that time, he was abused, suffered from starvation, cold, and beatings, saw his friends die, and, in the end, they shot him too. My mother, brother, and I had it hard during those years. I didn't think she'd ever come out of it. Finally, at the beginning of the 1940s, an uncle of ours, who had taken off to Cuba some time before, managed to get us there. Once in Havana, my mother sewed…or rather, she made hats for high society women. My brother and I were in charge of delivery and collection. I worked more because my brother was a deaf-mute. He passed away some time ago…"

He paused for a second, and sighed before continuing on:

"Anyway, it was hard during those years, and my mother decided to try our luck in New York. My uncle thought we were crazy, but it turned it out well. My mother—who would have imagined it—got married again to a man with an important job, and we were able to get an education. I studied electrical engineering, but I didn't pursue a career in it, rather I wound up working with technical translations. I got married, but Antonia and I didn't have any children. The poor thing. That caused her so much pain. Within just a few years, from 1970 to 1979, I lost my mother, stepfather, brother, and Antonia…and I found myself alone. New York was full of memories… Besides, I hated the cold. I sold everything, and I came here to Miami by the end of 1979."

Listening to his story, Maria was fascinated as she thought about how Cubans always spoke as if they were the only ones who had gone through a national calamity, and how this gentleman's story was like so many others'.

"I'm sorry. I didn't mean to recount my whole life. You're probably wondering what all of this has to do with Alberto, but it was a necessary introduction so that you can understand what happened later."

Just then, some bells began to ring without stopping.

"It's lunch time. Around here, Americans eat so early…at twelve. Would you like to stay? They allow me to have guests, but I'll warn you, the food's not that great."

Maria wasn't too sure. The invitation wasn't too appealing but she was so interested in his story that she decided to stay. Don Joaquin wasn't kidding. The fish with boiled potatoes and green beans couldn't have been more bland. The best part was the bread, the salad, and Jell-O with whipped cream for dessert. Worse still, they shared the table with two old chatterboxes and Mr. del Roble couldn't continue his story.

"I assume it's getting close to nap time. If you prefer, I can come back after four o'clock."

"Wonderful. I'll meet you back at the same place at four fifteen if that's ok," he said as he once again elegantly kissed her hand.

Maria had three hours to kill. Once in the car she looked over her emails on her phone. None of them was important except the one from Dr. Erwin. She opened it anxiously. It said that he had been able to extract DNA from a brush that they had found among the items belonging to Lazo, but that it would take more than two weeks before they had a definitive result. She sent him a reply, thanking him.

She couldn't decide whether to go over to the nearby shops at Dadeland or head back to the office… She decided instead to go see her father. On the way over, she stopped for a Cuban coffee to go… *Papi's coffee is terrible*, she thought to herself affectionately.

Her parents had always lived in the Westchester area, in the southwestern part of the city. It was a middle-class suburb where many Cubans had settled. Recently, there were also a lot of Hispanics from other countries too, so much so that there were hardly any Americans any more.

"Wow, well what a wonderful surprise," her father said as he greeted her with a sincere smile. She knew he was lonely, and she tried to take care of him the best she could.

The coffee had gotten cold, so her father warmed it up in the microwave, one of the few things in the kitchen he knew how to use. They sat there in silence, enjoying their coffee as well as each other's company.

She told him a bit about the case, but, without realizing it, she fell asleep in the recliner that her mother always used to sit in, and which despite all the years that had gone by still seemed to smell like her.

She woke up startled, fearing that she had slept through her appointment, but it was ok. She hadn't slept that long. She had just enough time touch up her hair and makeup and to hug her father goodbye.

Don Joaquin was waiting for her in the foyer. He was wearing a pullover sweater over the shirt he had been wearing that morning. Once they were settled back in the library, and she had turned on her tape recorder, he continued:

"As I was saying, I got to Miami at the end of 1979… I was getting to know the city, considering if I should buy a piece of property and where, deciding what to do with my life, when all that business at the Peruvian Embassy in Cuba took place in April 1980, followed by the Mariel Boatlift. Being Cuban, you no doubt remember it well…"

"Of course."

"Well, one day I get this call from this young man and he asks me if I'm from Villanueva de Jiloca… I thought it was strange that he knew what town I was from. He also asked about my brother, using his nickname Juancho—which is what we always called Juan—and I could tell he was upset when I told him that he had passed away. He told me his name was Alberto Gonzalez, that he had just arrived from Mariel, and that he needed to see me. He didn't tell me why. Since I'm usually a bit cautious, I didn't want to give him my address. I told him I'd meet him at a restaurant, some place where we could have a big lunch. Since he seemed reluctant, I told him I'd treat. He finally told me that he was staying at the camp in Tamiami Park, and he didn't have a penny to his name and didn't know how to get around. Even though I wasn't able to get it out of him why precisely he had called me, and I even imagined the worst, I went over to see him. You can't imagine my surprise when he told me that he was my brother's grandson… He told me that Juancho had had a daughter in Cuba and that for a while he used to send some money when he lived up in New York, but they hadn't heard from Juancho since the sixties. Alberto's mother was thirty-nine at the time, and he was nineteen. Alberto had taken off because he couldn't take it any longer. She had given him his grandfather's name as well as mine. Someone in the camp had helped him look up the numbers in the phone book and, on the third try calling one of the Robles, he came across mine."

"The truth is the whole thing seemed like a soap opera, but there was something about his features that reminded me of my brother. I also remembered a photo of a young girl that Juancho had in his wallet when he died, and tying up the loose ends and judging by the ages and dates, the whole story seemed to be more and more possible. Besides, the young man had good manners. He seemed sincere. So I made the necessary arrangements, which weren't many, and I got him out of there and took him to live with me. He turned out to be a godsend until… well…I don't want to get ahead of myself."

Don Joaquin kept coughing while he was talking and then explained that he had put on the sweater because he had a bit of a cold and they kept the air conditioning set very cold. After a while he had such a fit of coughing, he couldn't stop and he turned red. He couldn't breathe. Maria didn't know what to do. He took out a piece of candy, clumsily removed the wrapper and, once he started sucking on it, the cough went away little by little.

"Maybe you've overdone it today. I'm really interested in your story, a whole lot, but you have to take care of yourself… Maybe I should leave. Do you want me to call someone? Would you like me to accompany you to your room?"

Once he had recovered, he got up and looked at Maria with a mischievous smile.

"How about a drink? That's the best cure for a cough."

She was surprised by the English pub-style bar and the elegant music that was coming from the piano. A woman with a pronounced mouth moved her agile fingers over the keys from which one could hear notes from an ample repertoire, ranging from jazz to old *boleros*.

"She's really good. I'll introduce you later on," Don Joaquin promised, as he noticed Maria watching her intently.

"I always have a Scotch at this time of the day. I take mine neat. What you would like?"

"The same, but on the rocks."

They sipped their drinks in silence. This "old codger"—as Don Joaquin had referred to himself—stirred up Detective Duquesne's curiosity, admiration, and a certain sadness that she hoped wasn't going to turn into pity. It was a feeling that she preferred to reserve for innocent victims of so many crimes.

"So where were we?"

"You had agreed to be the sponsor for Alberto Gonzalez, and you had gotten him out of Tamiami…"

"Oh yes. Well, that led me to buy a small house, but one in a nice neighborhood…they call it West Gables…on Tangier Street. Are you familiar with the area?"

"Of course I am. It's very nice."

"While Alberto was studying English, I made arrangements to get a license and start a company selling alarms. In those days there were some incidents involving the boatlift people, or the 'Marielitos' as people called them. There weren't a lot. The majority turned out to be decent people, but simply put, people were scared and there was a lot of demand for alarms. The business took off. Alberto learned very quickly. I thought we should find a lawyer that could help take care of his status in the United States, but that was the only thing that he was never very clear about… He kept telling me that a friend of his had a lawyer who was going to fix everything, and that he had already taken care of the paperwork. The truth is that I should have been more on top of things. I've always respected the law. He gave me his social security number. I paid him through the payroll, and I seldom thought about it."

"Excuse me. The name on the social security, it was Alberto Gonzalez?"

"No. It was Raimundo Lazo. He explained that Raimundo Alberto was his given name and Lazo his maternal name, and that in filling out the forms the Alberto and the Gonzalez names had both somehow been deleted. These things happen in the United States all the time, so I didn't pay much attention to it."

Maria felt that her cellphone kept vibrating nonstop. She peeked at it and saw that it was Bill, her ex-husband. Fearful that something might have happened to Patrick, she excused herself and went to the bathroom where it was quieter and she could talk. She was relieved to find out that her son was fine. Bill had called just to complain about the expenses that had piled up with the beginning of Patrick's second year in college. She let him know abruptly that she was working and that they'd talk later.

When she returned, Don Joaquin was standing and waiting for her.

"They just called for dinner. I would invite you, but eating here twice in one day would be too much of a sacrifice for such a beautiful young woman as you…"

Maria could feel herself blush. Despite his years, Don Joaquin had not forgotten how to flirt with women.

Chapter 6

Day 3—Wednesday, November 4, 2015

The conversation with Bill couldn't have been more unpleasant. He had a good job as a company executive and made a lucrative salary, but he was an incredible cheapskate when it came to her and their son. All she had asked for was half the house in the divorce, and he had only agreed to pay the minimum court-ordered child support for Patrick until he finished high school, exactly one week after he turned eighteen. Nevertheless, their son's expenses continued… Fortunately, his grandfather had prepaid his tuition for any public university in Florida, and Patrick had worked a few hours a week to cover his personal expenses: phone bill, gas, gym membership, and dating. Maria didn't want him to graduate with the burden of student loans and insisted that she and Bill pay his rent and his car insurance and that they send him money for books and food. Once in a while, he had additional expenses like some car repairs or when he needed his wisdom teeth out—which were impacted—and, even worse, the health insurance didn't cover all the costs. Bill wound up paying half, but not without kicking and screaming. Each conversation between the two of them was always the same. Undoubtedly, as an American, his concept of family was different from the Hispanic one.

Although these conversations put her in a bad mood, Maria took comfort in the fact that at least she had the strength to go through with the divorce and, as time went by, she had to deal with him less often. At times, she couldn't understand how she'd been able to fall in love with a man like that. Had she just been blind or had Bill changed?

She wasn't in the mood to talk to anybody, so she decided to put on an old Orson Wells movie and was in bed by eleven o'clock.

Day 4—Thursday, November 5, 2015

She didn't sleep well. She had a nightmare in which she saw a man drowning in the sea whose remains then split into two identical parts that floated in the water.

As soon as she got to the office, she called Leo Adams to ask for an appointment to see him. Leo was a Cuban American lawyer who specialized in immigration cases. He was always busy but tended to see her immediately whenever she called. In exchange, she would cut through any red tape he might need in the Police Department.

Leo's office was on Flagler just in front of the courthouse, commonly called *Cielito Lindo*. According to her father, everyone referred to it by its nickname because there was a jail on the twenty-fourth floor and from there the prisoners could see the sky. She arrived an hour late. Traffic was getting worse all the time. She thought that the highest point on the Highway 836 bridge offered one of the prettiest views of the Miami. It was too bad she couldn't stop and enjoy it.

Leo didn't make her wait long, but he did interrupt their meeting a few times to answer the phone. His desk was covered with folders, papers, yellow sticky notes, and cigarette butts. Maria had already given up trying to convince him to quit smoking. Adams's secret for keeping so many clients with so few resources was to work on four or five things at a time with only one assistant.

Maria got him up to speed on the case:

"Supposedly, Alberto Gonzalez came on the Mariel Boatlift in 1980. He said he was from Cardenas, but I haven't confirmed that. He stole the identity of an American, named Ray Bow, who died that same year. He worked until 1992 as Raimundo Lazo using Bow's social security number. He died in '92. The car that he was driving fell into a canal. They never found the body of his young daughter, who was just a few weeks old. New evidence suggests that the subject might've been murdered. For starters, I don't know who he was. Can you help me?"

Leo lifted his eyes from his papers and looked at her.

"Do you know the exact date when he arrived, if he was in some kind of refugee camp, and if so who was his sponsor? Do you have a picture?"

"I don't know the exact date when he arrived, but maybe I can find out. I know that he was in Tamiami Park, and Joaquin de Roble was his sponsor. Here's Roble's past address and his current one. And here's a picture of the subject."

"You know, *El Nuevo Herald* has a database that can be accessed online, although if you don't know the exact name it can be tricky. I don't have enough staff to help you, but maybe someone in your department can do the search for you. However, if you want to sit down at that computer over there and try it yourself, I can help you if you run into trouble. It would be a lot faster…"

Since she didn't have anything urgent to do until she was supposed to go see the missing baby's grandmother that night, Maria spent the next two hours following Leo's instructions and going through the databases in order to find Alberto Gonzalez. She entered the birthdate on his license and the name Don Joaquin as the sponsor. She searched for Cardenas as his place of birth. She checked the names listed under Tamiami Park. Nothing.

At four o'clock, she waved goodbye and whispered thanks to Leo, who was on the phone, and she took off before the rush hour traffic got worse.

She had just enough time for a shower—she felt like her clothes wreaked of cigarette smoke from Leo's office—and to make herself a quick . smoothie of almond milk, yogurt, strawberries, and some protein powder that Patrick had given her. She drank it in front of the TV while she watched the ABC Evening News and then the beginning of *Wheel of Fortune*. She brushed her teeth, retouched her makeup, and set out for Hialeah.

She thought about her own grandmother and how she used to say that the pain endured by grandparents was twofold: they felt sorry for the problems of their grandchildren as well as their own children. She asked herself how a woman whose oldest granddaughter had disappeared at such a young age might feel, not knowing if the girl was dead or alive. Her first thought when she opened the door was that grandmothers these days were so different from those of years past.

Standing before her was a blonde woman (bleached, yes, but blonde nonetheless). She was dressed fashionably with a smart haircut and tasteful makeup. One could tell that she wasn't just a poor country person from Pinar del Rio. Although her face showed signs of age, it was obvious that she had been a beautiful young woman.

She greeted her kindly, invited her to have a seat, and offered her a cup of coffee.

Maria sat down but passed on the coffee. She preferred not to drink it at night. She started the same way she had with Gladys Elena, asking her if she was inclined to tell her the whole story again and to answer her questions honestly, even though she had done so a thousand times before. The woman agreed. Maria turned on her recorder and pulled out her notepad, then told her:

"Whenever you're ready, Mercedes."

"Mercy, call me Mercy, and don't be so formal, you'll make me feel old… Have you ever been to Pinar del Rio?"

"No, I'm sorry to say I was born here." The woman looked at her as though not being born in Cuba was a sin.

"It's beautiful…and it continues to be because the countryside is something that can't be stolen. The Valle de Viñales looks like no other place in the world. The whole province is beautiful and has a rich history ever since the War of Independence. Oh, sorry, I tend to prattle on… I was Spanish on my father's side. We were Asturian, so our life consisted of a small farm where we grew rice, tomatoes, potatoes, and

I don't know how many other things. Most people who live in that area were tobacco farmers, or *vegueros* as they're called there. They also grew henequen, which yields a lot but theirs was modest... My mother's family was of French descent. In Pinar del Rio, there are people from all over. Our neighbors were Lebanese... Mamá was a rural schoolteacher. You can't imagine all the jobs that came her way, but the truth is she didn't need the money. She only did it because it was her calling. In the province, education was important. Mamá showed me old photos of herself in a classroom with her students. She had to go on horseback... We lived in a house with a beautiful central patio, which is typical in those parts. Pinar del Rio is full of legends and music from songbirds."

"When did you get married?" Maria interrupted, hoping that the woman would start talking about things relevant to the case.

"Oh, sorry, it's just that no one wants to know about these stories, not even my children. I married very young, maybe when I was nineteen... I was born in '54. I was only five years old when the Revolution started. My family told me everything changed, but I believe that some things stayed the same... What I mean is that where there was once a pharmacy, there's still one; it's just that now it's falling down... When the agrarian reform came along, they tried to take the farm from my father, but we managed to keep a small part of it and stood up for ourselves. Supposedly, they made things somewhat better at my mom's school. Yeah right! They told her what she had to teach, but she fought back in the beginning since she had principles. So, by the time I came along, the teachers looked down on me. They called us *gusanos*, or worms, and even more so when my Uncle Jacinto left for the United States. In spite of that, I participated in all of the revolutionaries' activities. I went off to cut cane when I was only sixteen, and when I was eighteen I moved to Havana to go to school. I ran into even bigger problems when I was in college, mostly for making stupid remarks, because my cousin Jacinto Jose had been killed in Vietnam, fighting with the Americans. Someone said something about it, and since I am—or at least used to be—a loudmouth, I couldn't stand it and I told them off. So, I returned to Pinar del Rio because I was expelled from college... That's when I met Hilario. He was a decent *guajirote* from the country, polite, and

considerably refined for being a farmer. We fell in love, got married...
Gladys was born in '74, when I was twenty, and Raulito in '76. My
husband worked the land, I tended the house and raised the children,
and helped my mother at the school, where she still taught."

Mercy paused to offer her some mango juice. Maria accepted and the
woman came back with two glasses of the tropical nectar. They drank in
silence for a while until she started her story again.

"Now, where did I leave off? Ah, things began to get worse... Some of
the neighbors told Hilario to get on a raft and get out of Cuba. I always
thought that was crazy. Besides, I didn't want to leave my parents...
but when that *guajiro* got an idea into his head, he was more stubborn
than a mule. Finding materials and constructing the raft in secret was
a real undertaking, as you know. You have to understand that I love my
children, but I just couldn't get on that raft with them. I had a panic
attack when I saw the blackness of the sea...there was no moon...
it was an imposing darkness. I didn't believe that Hilario would do it,
but our neighbors were pressuring him to leave. The thing is, they got
onto the raft, pushed off, and I stayed on the shore as still as a statue.
The ten days I waited without hearing from them were the longest of
my life. At last, Gladys called me crying a river to tell me that her father
had drowned, and our neighbor and his wife too. My children were the
only ones who made it. The Virgin had protected them because of all of
my prayers."

She appeared exhausted after retelling this part of her story. She looked
for a Kleenex and wiped her nose.

"I nearly went crazy thinking about my children, all alone. I haven't
even told this to my children, but it's the only time in my life that I have
borrowed money. I called my Uncle Jacinto in New York. He really
came through. I had to pay eight thousand dollars to get there in a
boat, because there's was no way I could do it on a raft. But don't think
that the boat was an easy trip. It went quickly. Seated in the bottom of
the boat with the other passengers, you could feel the waves from the
bottom all the way up to the top of your head. I didn't get seasick or

vomit like the others did. Maybe because I was focused on praying…
But sometimes I thought that I couldn't put up with it anymore. It
was daylight when we came ashore on an island. Then the coast guard
picked us up. In the end, it was quite a journey. They detained me in
Key West for a few days, but when I finally got to embrace my children,
I knew that it had all been worth it."

"And what can you tell me about Raimundo Lazo?"

"Well, I really didn't have that many dealings with him. They left
Cuba on October 15—can you believe it? In the middle of hurricane
season?—and I arrived here at the end of December. He and my
daughter were already dating. I didn't approve. She had left a boyfriend
back in Cuba, a decent boy who we had known for his whole life.
And she was so young! But when I tried to give my opinion, they told
me that they had already gotten married by a judge and that she was
pregnant. They said that she was due in October and later on said that it
was two months premature, but I knew it was just a cover-up—she was
already pregnant when they got married… What could I do? And these
days, what does it matter? Later, as you know, she ended up marrying
the boyfriend from Pinar del Rio."

"Yes…but what did you think of Lazo?"

"Well, I've never told anyone this before because it's a difficult feeling to
describe…but I didn't like that man at all… I can't tell you why exactly."

"Did he treat your daughter well?"

"Like a princess… He seemed quite in love with her."

"Did he drink, or do drugs, or was he impolite?"

"No, nothing like that, he was respectful, always around, and
very attentive."

"Then what didn't you like about him?"

"I'm not sure… He gave me the impression that he was
hiding something."

"What makes you think so?"

"I'm not sure… It's been a long time… I just had my suspicions."

"And do you believe that your granddaughter is alive?" Maria
asked unexpectedly.

"Sometimes yes. Sometimes I am certain she is and can almost feel her
presence. Other times no. It seems like none of this happened and that
it was all a dream…or a nightmare. But I have to tell my daughter that I
am sure that she's alive, or it's going to kill her. If I thought I was going
to go crazy when they were on the raft and didn't know if they had
arrived safely, and it was only for a few days, imagine waiting all these
years! You understand that Duquesa?"

"Duquesne is my last name. Yes, I understand. I don't want to take up
any more of your time. It's late and I know you work, but if possible I
might want to see you again."

"Anytime you need to…don't hesitate to call me."

"Please think hard about why it seemed like Lazo was hiding
something," Maria said in the doorway.

And just as her daughter had done, Mercy said goodbye to Detective
Duquesne with a kiss on the cheek.

Chapter 7

Day 4—Thursday, November 5, 2015

As soon as she got in her car, Maria felt her stomach growl. Undoubtedly, the smoothie she had drunk wasn't going to hold her over. She remembered there was a restaurant—La Carreta—in the Hialeah area. According to her GPS, it was close, so she decided to stop for something to eat. She got in line for the carry out window to ask for a *medianoche* sandwich to take back home, but she thought she recognized someone inside and decided to go in instead. She looked for a table where she could go unnoticed, and she hid her face behind the menu. At first, she had her doubts, but it didn't take her long to become convinced that she was looking at Ramon Morales, Lourdes's husband. He was sitting with a young woman, and they were chatting animatedly. What was a man who lived in Coral Gables doing in Hialeah at this hour? Was her mother's friend right that her husband was hiding something? There had to be a better explanation, she told herself. She also knew that she couldn't spy on him, but if it happened to be a chance encounter, that was different.

The waitress came by. She ordered quickly. As soon as the woman left, Maria noticed that Ramon paid the bill and stood up with the girl. She had already given back her menu, so she didn't have any way to hide her face. They were going to go right past her. She wasn't sure whether to greet him or to get up and go to the bathroom. She didn't have time to decide. Lourdes's husband was already too close. Then she heard a cell phone ring and saw Ramon reach into his pocket to answer it, and he put his head down just as he passed her table. He had not seen her! She thought about following them. Her curiosity was piqued, but it was against department regulations to act as a private detective. Still, if no one paid her, it was a bit different… Besides, no one had to know. She doubted it would amount to much, and when she opened the door, she saw Ramon's car driving away. However, it looked like he was alone.

If that was the case, he had met the young woman there, and she had her own car. She thought about heading out and seeing if she saw the woman and taking down her license plate number, but she decided not to. Maybe in the back of her mind she preferred not to know what Ramon was up to.

She left half of the *medianoche* because she had quickly lost her appetite. She didn't sleep too well that night, so in spite of her standard morning Cuban coffee, she was sleepy when she arrived at the station.

Day 5—Friday, November 6, 2015

"You have a message on your desk," one of her fellow officers told her when she entered.

It seemed strange to her that someone she didn't know had called from The Palace. She immediately dialed the number. They told her that they were calling on behalf of Don Joaquin. He had been hospitalized for a lung condition, and she wouldn't be able to see him for a few days. She practically had to beg them to tell her that he was in Kendall Medical Center.

"But he's not allowed to have any visitors," the woman on the other end of the phone warned.

Regardless, Maria went to the hospital to try to see him. When she identified herself as a police officer and assured them that it would only take a few minutes, they let her in. Don Joaquin looked thinner than when she had last seen him, like a small, fragile bird between the sheets. He was on oxygen, and a nurse was in the process of taking his vitals. Even though the thermometer in his mouth prevented him from saying anything, his eyes showed that he was happy to see her.

When they were alone, Maria asked him not to talk; he needed to rest so that he could recover quickly and then tell her the rest of his story. They must have given him a sedative, because the old man smiled peacefully and fell asleep right away.

When she got back to the station, Detective Duquesne reviewed all of her case notes. Suddenly, she got up and knocked on her boss's office door.

"Larry, I need to talk to you."

Her tone was serious, and Lawrence Keppler lifted his glance from the papers he was reading and listened attentively.

"Look, one of the main problems we have to solve in this case is that we don't know the identity of the person who died in the car that fell into the canal. He used a fake name and social security number, and there is no trace of him anywhere, not even in the Department of Immigration."

"What do you propose we do?"

"I think we need to try to get the cooperation of the Cuban government."

"You're crazy! You know how unreasonable Captain Rios is. If you tell him that, God knows how he'll react."

"I know or, at least, I think I know, but our professional work has to come before our ideological differences. Now that there is more collaboration on a few matters between the two countries, it shouldn't be too difficult to send the photo and the DNA, and for them to tell us his real name and if he had a criminal record. This man is obviously hiding something, and I think the sooner we find out, the sooner we can solve this case."

"And what do you think happened?"

"You know that it's not good to make conjectures until we have all the facts."

"But you've always had a great instinct, and sometimes the nose of an investigator is her best weapon."

"Fine, I could be wrong, and it's very premature, but my nose—as you say—tells me that it wasn't an accident, that they killed him, but I don't know why or who."

"And the little baby?"

"I think she's alive, and if that's true, we need to find her."

"Ok, give me a few days, and I'll see if we can get the cooperation of the Cuban government, but I don't think the DNA will do us much good. When he left in 1980, they didn't even use DNA to solve cases in the US, much less in Cuba. If you at least had his fingerprints, it would help."

"I'll keep looking, but the cooperation of the Cuban government could be crucial. Thanks so much."

She went back to her desk and again plunged into the databases within her reach but couldn't find any Alberto Gonzalez who would have come through Mariel with the same birthdate. Then it dawned on her that if he used a fake name and social security number, the birthdate could be fake too. It might have belonged to Ray Bow and not Alberto Gonzalez. She pulled up the information on four people by that same name, all who had arrived through Mariel. Two were small children, so she ruled them out. One was much older, age seventy. The fourth was born in 1963. That would have made him seventeen when he arrived, two years younger than the age on Raimundo Lazo's papers.

She called Leo. His assistant answered, and she had to wait a few minutes before he came to the phone. She cut right to the chase:

"Leo, were minors under eighteen treated differently in Tamiami if they arrived alone?"

"You told me he was nineteen."

"Yes, but I think the papers were falsified, and he was only seventeen."

"They wouldn't have let him leave the camp so easily if he were that young."

"Wait, have you ever heard of anyone in the area who falsified documents?"

"I've heard rumors but have never been able to verify them."

"Who would know?"

"The only person that comes to mind would be Manuel Larrea."

"The writer?"

"Yes, he came through Mariel, and I think he talked about it in one of his novels, but maybe it was all fictitious. He lives in Miami Beach."

"You're a gem, Leo. I owe you one."

Maria again felt that inner tingling sensation that came with a new clue.

Next, she searched for Larrea's books on Amazon. She learned that his novel about the Mariel Boatlift was out of print and copies sold for $175 each. She decided to call him instead and arranged to meet him the next day at his apartment in South Beach.

Chapter 8

Day 5—Friday, November 6, 2015

Maria woke up with one of those migraines that barely lets you move your head or tolerate the light. Still, she didn't waste a single minute. She made some Cuban coffee and took two Excedrin. Then she got in the shower, adjusted the nozzle to increase the pressure, and soaked her head under the stream for a long while. As she dried her hair with a towel, she firmly pressed on her temples and pressure points.

When she got to the office, she felt better but didn't feel up to driving all the way to Miami Beach. She saw Fernandez at his desk. He was a young man who hadn't been on the force for very long. Larry had told her to ask for help if she needed it, so she stuck her head in his office and asked him if she could take the rookie with her to an interview.

Fernandez was delighted. On their way to Miami Beach, he couldn't stop talking about the case and asking Maria questions. She was almost sorry she had asked him to come along.

She was caught off guard when Larrea opened the door. She was barely in high school when the Mariel Boatlift happened, but she remembered him as he was in 1980 when he had just arrived and had just published his novel. He had appeared a few times in the press. Back then he was a handsome, young man with a dark, bushy beard. Now, his hair, mustache, and the few remaining whiskers in his beard had all turned totally white. He had also put on some weight. Maria realized that thirty-five years had gone by, which was how old the writer must have been in the photos she remembered. He was probably near seventy now. When he smiled and stared back at her with his green eyes, she recognized a glimmer of the man she remembered.

"I'm Ivan Fernandez," the young policeman was the first one to speak and to hold his hand out effusively to the author. "And she's the boss, Detective Maria Duquesne."

She was a bit irritated by her subordinate's initiative, but it was true that she had been dumbstruck by an image that she hadn't expected.

"Please, sit down… My place is rather small, and the imps are always rearranging things, but I combat them with a bunch of *güijes*. Do you know what *güijes* are?"

"Sure, they're…nymphs or some type of fairy in Cuban folklore."

Maria was surprised by Fernandez' immediate reply. Maybe it was good she had brought him along. She didn't have the slightest idea of what a güije was or if Larrea was pulling their leg.

"We're here because we've reopened a case about a young man who came through Mariel and who died in 1992. We thought that maybe you could clear up a few things for us. First, although it would be a miracle, by chance do you recognize the person in these photos?"

Larrea looked carefully at the two pictures Maria had handed him.

"I don't know. There are so many Cubans and Hispanics with a dark complexion like that… Well, not me so much, since I inherited my great-grandfather's green eyes. He reminds of someone, but I can't put my finger on it… No, I don't think I know him. What happened to him?"

Maria told him how they had found him in the canal and about the missing baby, but she didn't tell him about the falsified documents or about the suspicion that he had been murdered.

"So how can I be of service?"

Maria sensed that maybe the question had a double meaning and that it was directed more at Fernandez than her, but she didn't understand completely.

"I wanted you to tell me a little about leaving Cuba, your arrival in Key West, your stay in the Orange Bowl and in Tamiami Park, because I know that he was in both places."

Larrea closed his eyes, opened them a moment later, and then got to his feet.

"Darling, it would take me more than a lifetime to tell you the whole story!"

There was such a dramatic tone to his voice that she was grateful when Fernandez intervened.

"We understand that completely. I've read your novel, and I know the whole story isn't even there, but maybe to help us out in this case you could try and give us some broad ideas."

Larrea and Fernandez exchanged glances for a brief second, and then Maria realized what was going on. They were both gay, and the seventy-something writer and the young policeman were dancing a minuet. They were sizing up their powers of seduction and intrigue. She was just about to get up and leave but instead decided to take advantage of the situation.

"Look, Larrea, it's just that besides being interested in this particular case, Fernandez was telling me the whole way over here how much he admires you, and what an honor it was going to be to meet you, and what it would mean to hear your statement from your own voice... So, if you don't mind, I'd like to record if that's ok."

Larrea leaned back in his armchair. All of a sudden, it was as if he were rejuvenated.

"Well, in that case... Look, in 1980, Cuba was a pressure cooker. In the previous year, some of the people who had left in the beginning went back to visit, the ones that the government had called a plague and had said how badly it had gone for them... However, they were all overweight and rich (or at least that's what they said), and everybody either envied them or hated them, or at times both. In Cuba in those days, life amounted to interminable speeches, fear from denunciations, the daily absurdity of it all, meetings, volunteer work, inefficiency, prohibitions. There was a long list of things you couldn't do, like wear long hair or listen to the Beatles, and other things that you couldn't be, like a homosexual for example. In the sixties, they all wound up in the UMAP camps where the government had sent them to be cured! After that came the events at the Peruvian Embassy. I don't think it ever dawned on Fidel that ten thousand people were going to squeeze into that house in Miramar. Everybody in Cuba wanted out. So, he told them to get out! But it came with a price. He made it so that those who were leaving would have to swallow their pride."

Maria was familiar with similar stories, but she had never heard them directly from the mouth of one of the protagonists. Despite all the years, the writer's wounds still hadn't healed. He began to speak more and more passionately, waiving his hands around as if they too wanted to express their indignation.

"If you could have only seen everyone swearing that they were prostitutes, pimps, queers, murderers, begging on their knees for them to stamp their papers. People took off without saying goodbye, without even getting a toothbrush, without an address or telephone number of someone they could call once they arrived, without knowing what it's like to be a refugee, without knowing that their lives had just been split into two no matter how bad what they were leaving behind had been, without thinking, because the only thing they felt in every muscle, in every pore in their skin, was the need to flee… And then came the hours in the camp, El Mosquito, without any place to take a piss or shit, and those dogs that you thought were going to attack you. And later on those boats crammed with people, and that stench of sweat and vomit, those sobs, and cries, and prayers…until you finally saw the coast, and even though we had lost the feeling in our legs we stepped onto the wharf, and some men in uniform took us by the arm, and they smiled at us and told us 'Welcome to the USA,' and they gave us a Coke and sandwiches and apples, some of us had never seen an apple before, and then they put us on a bus, or at least that's what happened to me, and they took us to a stadium where they gave us cots, and cartons with toothbrushes, toothpaste, and things like that. People were dumbfounded, as equally thrilled as they were tired, absolutely exhausted as if they had never slept before, and then they began to call out names from a list, and they finally called mine, and they put me on another bus, and they took me to another camp where they began to ask me things and take down information until I found a relative, and it really was a miracle but he came looking for me and took me out for a steak and a beer and he told me, 'Hell, Manny, you're finally free!' And you know, in moments like those, damn, you don't know what to make of it, of being free. It makes you dizzy. You don't know how to be free because you never, never had the chance to choose."

He was exhausted, and Maria could see that Fernandez's eyes had teared up.

"That's a very moving story," Maria commented. "Look, do you remember if they took your fingerprints in Tamiami Park?"

"I think so. Yes, I'm almost certain."

"And do you remember if there was someone, maybe among those who came or maybe who was already there, who was in the business of falsifying documents?"

Larrea smiled.

"You know that where there are three Cubans, there's at least one shady person."

"But do you remember someone in particular?"

"Yeah, there was a couple, a man and a woman…they were like everybody else, but when they got close to people and saw that they were worried…"

"Worried? Why?"

"Well, for a lot of reasons…maybe they had a criminal file back in Cuba and they were afraid they weren't going to let them in, maybe they had been a member of the militia or even a member of the party until the previous day, maybe they were minors or didn't have family here who could sponsor them. There were so many things that they wanted to cover up."

"And do you remember anything else about this couple, maybe someone whom they helped?"

"As I told you, they were just ordinary folks…and it was so long ago. But he went by some nickname… I don't know, Tiger, Gimpy, Monkey… I don't know. Those types of nicknames are so common in Cuba… I don't remember."

"Try. Please," Fernandez pleaded. "Go ahead, at least for me, since it's one of my first cases."

"Well, if you leave your number, and I can remember, I'll call you."

No sooner had Maria given him her card than Fernandez offered his as well. Larrea looked at it, gently ran his index finger over it, and placed it in his wallet.

"I'll keep it right here so the fairies won't hide it. I promise I'll try to remember. Sometimes things come to me when I'm sleeping… How strange, right?"

Maria got up to leave. When they were already at the door, Larrea put his hand on her shoulder.

"Wait. I just remembered something else. That couple helped a friend of mine that had some type of problem or another. His name is Jacinto… Jacinto Bengochea… He's a writer, and he lives in New York. Wait just a minute and I'll go get his number."

Chapter 9

Days 6 and 7—Saturday and Sunday, November 7 and 8, 2015

After lunch, Maria had almost fallen asleep watching a rerun of *Law and Order* when she heard the lock on her front door begin to open. Only her father, her son, and a neighbor had the key, and she was just about to take out her pistol when the door opened, and she saw Patrick in the doorway.

"*Mijo*, what are you doing here?"

"Mami, I got up early and drove all the way here without stopping. I don't have class on Monday until late in the afternoon. I came down to spend the weekend with you."

"That's wonderful, but it couldn't be that there's some party tonight or that you want to see some girl, could it?"

"Well, maybe that too…" Her son's smile lit up the living room, which he had reached with just two big leaps, and then he gave her such a big hug that it almost took her breath away.

"Don't tell anyone, but I felt a little homesick."

"Well, let me know next time."

"If you have plans," he said with a sly expression, "I can go to *abuelo*'s house."

"No…I wish! I just like to know when you're on the road."

"Just so you can worry about me?"

"Well, yes, and so I can have more food in the house…"

"Don't worry about it. Give me some money, and I'll go do the shopping."

"Well, how kind of you! *Este huevo quiere sal.*"

"You sound just like *abuelo* with all those Cuban sayings."

"You know very well what that means."

"Yeah. *This egg wants salt.*"

"No, *you want something.*"

"Don't be so negative, Mami. I don't need money… Look, it's true that there happens to be a party tonight over at Pete's house, and I was missing my friends here, and some others have come home too, but tomorrow I'll spend all day with you and *abuelo*. If you want to, we can go out to eat, but the truth is I'm dying for some of your chicken and rice. Oh man! And sweet plantains too, even if they're the frozen ones from Publix."

"Your grandfather would love that. I'll call him right now."

The weekend was a constant coming and going of all of Patrick's friends. Finally, at noon on Sunday her father arrived with all the ingredients: chicken legs and thighs marinated in Sazón Badía, one large onion, green pepper, Valencia rice, tomato sauce, roasted peppers, olives, and enough beer to boil the rice and for them to drink too.

"You have *bijol*, don't you?" he asked before anything else.

"Of course I do, Papi. What Cuban kitchen would be without annatto spice? And I have all the other spices you could want: oregano, bay leaves, garlic salt…"

"Ok, fine."

The truth is that Patricio could have never prepared an entire dish of chicken and rice by himself, but he helped his daughter, just as he had always done with his wife, and both of them pretended that he was the better chef.

"Let's see. Taste the broth. You think it needs some salt?" While they cooked, they drank some Coronas, ate some pork rinds, and listened to a record by Albita. They danced, they laughed. Father and daughter hugged at times and, at others, they looked the other way so the other wouldn't notice that their eyes had teared up. It didn't matter that six years had gone by and that her mother would have never been in this particular house or kitchen. They still felt her presence and it hurt and, at the same time, it was an immense comfort like the taste of candy after taking bitter medicine.

They had just put the lid on the pot and lowered the heat on the boiling water for the rice when Maria's cellphone rang. *Don't let it be an emergency down at the station. Don't let anyone kill anybody today*, was her first thought.

It wasn't a call from work. It was Yolanda, her mother's friend. She was speaking so softly that Maria couldn't understand her at first. Finally, she made out that Ramon had taken off for the weekend, that Lourdes was still convinced that he was cheating on her, that she was very depressed, and she didn't know what to do to cheer her up.

"Well, why don't you come on over? Papi and I are cooking up some chicken and rice, and Patrick came in yesterday. Of course, there's enough. No, no, don't bring anything, but come over right away because the rice will be ready in a half hour, and we should eat it as soon as it's done."

Her father gave her a look as if he were saying "you're hopeless."

"Papi, they were so good to Mami. They care for us a lot, and they feel so alone these days…and what difference does it make since you and Patrick are going to wind up talking about sports?"

The "crazy" women arrived just as Maria was setting the table and finishing up the rice. Patrick came out of his room, fresh out of the shower, and doused with a half bottle of cologne. *Look how handsome my son is*, Maria thought to herself. And, as if the adopted aunts had read her mind, they all began to sing his praises.

"He's gotten even taller…"

"And his shoulders have gotten broader."

"You're going to catch all the ladies like that!"

Patrick gave them a kiss with a big smile. It must have taken care of Lourdes's depression because they spent the whole afternoon drinking, eating, telling jokes, and playing dominos as if it were a holiday.

Chapter 10

Days 8 and 9—Monday and Tuesday, November 9 and 10, 2015

No one had to tell her that something had happened. Maria knew as soon as she set foot in the station that another crime had occurred. She immediately rushed to Larry's office to offer her help.

"As much as I want you to close the case I assigned to you, we need all hands on deck right now. Head into the conference room. I'll be there in a minute, and we'll bring you up to speed."

She soon learned that they had found the body of a young Hispanic man in a wooded area of Homestead. Everyone got moving. There were officers at the crime scene right away, some overseeing the collection of forensic evidence, others questioning possible witnesses, and two of them talking to family members, the hardest task of all. They asked Maria to interview the victim's brother, who had stumbled upon the dead body. They always had to rule out family as suspects. Even though many years of working as a police detective had toughened Maria, violence against children and young people still upset her. The dead boy was seventeen, even younger than her son Patrick. They gave her two pictures: the first was of a round-faced boy with olive skin, large glasses, and a broad smile. In the second one, the same face was almost unrecognizable. His head had been sliced open, badly damaging his forehead and part of his left eye. The preliminary forensic reports showed that there were at least fifteen deep machete wounds.

The first thing she concluded was that this couldn't have been the work of one single person. When she saw Pedro Guarda—a trembling, scrawny young man, who was barely five feet tall—she was positive that he hadn't been involved in this brutal murder. She tried to calm him down and get some more information. When he stopped crying, Pedro told her that his brother had participated in the Job Corps program to finish high school and learn a trade. His parents were Mexican, and they had worked multiple jobs, mostly in agriculture. When they were little, they lived with their grandmother back in their hometown. Their mother and father would cross the border, work for a few months, send money back to support them, and then they would be with them when they didn't have work. But since their grandmother was getting old, and crossing the border was becoming increasingly difficult, their parents brought them to the United States. When things got bad in Arizona, they piled in their rundown truck with all of their belongings and drove straight through to Homestead. Their father had a friend there, and he started working in agriculture right away. He would have preferred a construction job, but there weren't any. Their mother cleaned houses there, and that's how they got by.

"We're illegals," he said with such a deep sadness that Maria felt the urge to hug him. "I have a teacher who says that no one is really illegal, that we're simply undocumented immigrants which is not the same thing, but for the sake of the case…"

"I'm older, I should have protected my little brother…" he said and started weeping again.

"It's not your fault, Pedro," Maria said, trying to console him.

He continued:

"Jose took after my mother. He had a weight problem that really got worse when we came to this country. I went to that same high school program last year, and I definitely learned a lot. They helped me find the job I have now as a plumber's assistant, but Jose was going through a hard time. Other students made fun of him. You know, those bullies that are at every school. More than once, I got into fistfights to defend him. I also told him that he should start working out to lose weight, but my mother always said that we didn't have the money for special diets, and we'd have to keep eating the same stuff. And I don't know, I guess the worse things got, the more my brother would eat."

"And those kids who bullied him, do you know their names?"

Pedro shook his head, and his dark eyes filled with tears once again. Maria noticed that he was biting his lip and his fists were clenched. He kept quiet for a few minutes.

"I can assure you that they will never know that you were the one that gave me their names."

She took out a pen and a notepad and placed them on the table in front of him.

"The names, Pedro, please."

The boy sat still.

"Look, I'm scared that they'll deport us over this. It's very sad, but perhaps it's better to just let it go."

"Do you think your brother deserved that death? And if they kill others? What if they do the same to you?"

Pedro finally wrote down the names of four boys and one girl. They all had criminal records, although not for violent crimes, and they soon found evidence that proved their guilt.

After they were arrested and interrogated separately, each one told the same story and with the same tone, as if they were all narrating the same exact movie that seemingly had nothing to do with them. A few days before they had dug a hole and buried a machete. That Friday night they arranged to meet Jose in the forest. They told him that if he was a real man he needed to prove it by smoking pot with them and having sex with a girl that they were going to bring, so they could see whether he was a fag or what… Jose showed up, and they took turns slashing him with the machete, not very hard at first, to see what his blood looked like. Later on, they told him to lie down in the hole, and that the girl was going to take off her clothes and get on top of him to see if he was a man or not. That's when Jose tried to resist; he didn't want to get in the hole, and Mikel lost it. He hit Jose so hard with the machete that his skull cracked in two, and he died.

"It was a shame," said one of the suspects, "because we could've had a little more fun with him. I missed the first part because I had walked away to take a piss."

Then they all helped bury him. They cleaned up the blood and took the machete and hid it far away. They all went to get some pizza, except for Mikel and Queenie, who stayed back there to have sex because he was really horny and couldn't wait.

The girl was the only one who resisted when they arrested her. She headbutted an officer in the chest and slapped him in the face before they were able to put her in handcuffs.

In forty-eight hours, all five of them had been arrested and had appeared before a judge. All were going to be tried as adults.

When she got back home after two days of barely any sleep, Maria took a long shower and went to bed without eating. That bloody orgy had been much worse than anything she had read in *Lord of The Flies* as a teenager, and it made quite an impression on her. Each time she thought of the crime scene, with the mutilated corpse of the young Mexican boy, and imagined his last moments, she gagged uncontrollably and had to run to the bathroom to vomit.

Chapter 11

Day 10—Wednesday, November 11, 2015

Maria had finished all the reports about the Homestead case and was preparing to review her notes on Raimundo Lazo and his daughter when they forwarded a call to her:

"It's a woman who says she lost your business card. I can't tell if it's a joke or not. She asked for the Duchess. She said to tell you it was Mercy."

It only took Maria a few seconds to figure out that it was the missing baby's grandmother who was trying to reach her.

"What can I do you for you, Mercedes?"

"Oh, *hija*, it's been such a headache trying to reach you! I lost your business card. That's what happens when I hide things so well that I can't find them… I even invoked Saint Dimas by tying a cloth to the leg of a chair, but it still hasn't shown up. Here's the thing, I have a person that I think you should speak with. Do you have something to write with?"

"Yes, I'm ready."

"Her name is Rosa, Rosa Blass. She used to have a store in Miami Beach, but she's much older now, maybe over ninety. But still very clear-minded."

"What was her relationship to your son-in-law?"

"She told me that he used to stop by the store quite often and they'd talk. The truth is she mentioned that to me years ago but I had just forgotten, and then yesterday she called me out of the blue—I have to believe in mysterious forces, telepathy, whatever—and before I could get a word in she began talking about Ray… I asked her if she would mind if you called her sometime soon, and she told me to give you her number, so here it is."

Maria was very interested in following up on the lead that Larrea had given her about calling his colleague the writer, but she had a feeling that the man wouldn't speak on the phone, and she first needed to know if Larry would cover the costs to travel to New York to interview him. She didn't think she could leave it in the hands of the NYPD, so she decided to call Rosa Blass and arrange an appointment. Her daughter answered, and Maria had to give her multiple explanations for why she wanted to see her mother until she heard a nasally voice in the background say, "It's for me, *hija*, Mercy told me that the detective was going to call. I want to speak with her."

Rosa Blass picked up the phone and agreed for Maria to come by her apartment in Miami Beach at four o'clock that afternoon. All the roads that went to the beach seemed to lead to another world, and Maria especially enjoyed the view of the ocean on either side of the highway and the silhouette of Miami Beach as she got closer.

After traveling for an hour, Maria came to the town of Surfside, home to many different economic classes and ethnic groups but mostly white. The wealthiest people lived in the tall condominium buildings like the one where she arrived precisely at four in the afternoon. When the doorman confirmed that they were expecting her, she went through an opulent lobby and took the elevator to the eighteenth floor. On the doorframe, she noticed a *mezuzah*—a small, oblong box where Jewish people hang scrolls with verses from the Torah. A few seconds later, a middle-aged woman opened the door and invited her to come in and take a seat.

The living room had a breathtaking ocean view, and it was decorated with high quality, modern furniture and a huge oil painting by the Cuban painter Baruj Salinas. There were many silver frames that showed off family photos: some old black and white ones, and more recent ones in color. The marble floors were impeccably polished.

On one of the sidewalls, a large bookcase housed many well-kept, organized volumes.

Down the hallway she heard the voice of the woman who had opened the door, and clearly someone else was with her.

"Here comes Mrs. Blass."

Rosa walked in, supported by a walker, but she moved with surprising agility. She acknowledged Maria with her head and sat in an armchair. She had her hair dyed dark brown and on her broad forehead she had thick eyebrows, an alert gaze, a half smile, and skin with some freckles and fewer wrinkles than one would expect for a woman her age. She didn't have that fragility that just a few days ago Maria had noticed in the exiled Spaniard when she visited him in the hospital. Maria saw the signs of age primarily on her hands.

"I've just turned ninety-six."

That was the first thing Rosa Blass said, as if presuming that Maria was adding up the years from the signs that might give away her old age.

"But my mind and memory are clear," she continued, with the nasally voice in which you could hear the almost indiscernible influence of another language.

"What a pleasure it is to meet you, Rosa. You seem to be in such good health."

"Thank you, my dear. Would you like something to drink? Yadiris can make us something. She's Cuban and hasn't been here too long, but she takes great care of me. Although she's a horrible cook," she whispered to Maria in a soft voice, using her hand to cover up what she was saying.

Faced with Rosa's insistence, she accepted an iced tea, and Yadiris placed two glasses next to them.

As usual, Maria took out her tape recorder, notebook, and pen, and asked permission to record their conversation.

"Of course, I'm not going to reveal any war secrets to you," said Rosa.

Maria was impressed that this almost one-hundred-year-old woman was still elegant and had a sense of humor.

"What can you tell me about Raimundo Alberto Lazo?" Maria asked without preface.

"Let's see…we went into exile in 1960… Well…the second exile, because my parents went to Cuba from Poland in 1928…but not as refugees. They were fleeing poverty and lack of opportunities, and a special kind of misfortune that followed my poor father. I was just a little girl, but I have many memories from that rough time in my life. There were five of us sisters…you can imagine how difficult it was to feed such a large family… I can tell you more about that period in my life another day. In Cuba my parents went through tons of different jobs, like all immigrants do, but they did ok, and my sisters and I did even better… Then, you know what happened with the start of the Revolution. We left immediately, in 1960, and first we came to Miami with our daughters. The oldest was already married, and the youngest got married here. Next we spent a few years in Puerto Rico, but we returned to Miami where we had lots of friends. The idea was for us to retire, but my husband didn't know how to go about life with nothing to do, and so he opened two stores on Lincoln Road. I didn't want to get involved, but you know how it is… Little by little I started spending more time helping out at the stores."

"Was that where you met Lazo?" Maria asked.

"No. We closed those stores sometime in the mid-seventies, but my daughter Sara had another store, and, even though I had sworn not to work anymore, I used to spend a few hours helping out there each week, and when she would travel to New York to buy clothes, I would spend the entire day at the store. She had great employees, but I had to keep an eye on things. Even more so at that time, because after Mariel, people who hung out at the beach started to change. But Ray was not one of those. He was a good guy."

"Did he buy things at the store?"

"Well, not very often, only occasionally. But he would stop by now and then."

"Why?" Maria asked.

"I think he would meet up with people in the coffee shop next door."

"Do you know who?"

"No."

"You never saw him talking with them?"

"Well, now that you're picking my brain, actually, yes I did. One time these people came into the store and bought something. It was a man and a woman. I think they were married or at least a couple. You know how things are these days."

"Do you remember anything about them? Their names? What they looked like?"

"It's been so many years. You're talking about the eighties…when he first got here. But although they seemed to be friends, I was under the impression that these meetings always made Ray nervous and that they were exchanging something… I don't know, I don't think that he was selling or buying drugs or anything like that, but they definitely didn't seem like normal visits between friends."

"And how frequently would they meet there?"

"Like once a month, maybe every six weeks."

"Did Ray ever tell you anything about his life?"

"He kept to himself but was still very nice. He told me that he worked with an uncle installing alarms, but he said very little about his life in Cuba. Oh…and he told me that he liked to write. Sometimes while waiting, he would write something down in a notebook that he almost always had on him."

"And about when did these meetings stop taking place?"

"I would have to ask Sara which year exactly she sold the store… And after that I didn't really see him anymore until I ran into him with Mercy in a shopping center."

"When did you meet Mercy?"

"I met her in Cuba, while we were on vacation in Pinar del Rio. Later she came to visit me in Havana. She's much younger than me. Actually, her mother was more my age, but she died a while ago. She was a teacher, and in that little schoolhouse in Pinar del Rio she taught math to one of my sisters. I didn't recognize Mercy when I first saw her again in Miami, but she recognized me. She had already arrived from Cuba, and her daughter was married to Ray. We would talk on the phone every now and again… You know, people like to talk with others who remember their parents and their lives back home."

"Is there anything else you can tell me about the couple that Ray would meet with?"

"I don't know, they seemed pretty normal…they didn't appear to be that classy…he usually looked worse than she did."

"You don't remember their names, not even their last name?"

"No…well, one thing… I don't know if this is of any importance. It was a few days before Halloween, and Sara had put kids' costumes on sale. There were various popular ones, of Michael Jackson and also a doll… And another one of a bear. It was a smiling bear, you know, for little kids. She took it in her hands and showed it to him, and said, 'Look, if they had your size it would be perfect for you.' He looked at her like he wanted to kill her and responded with some four-letter word because he saw himself as a bad-ass and not cute like that bear mask."

"Do you think they called him 'El Oso'?"

"That's definitely a possibility."

When Maria returned home from the beach, Miami gave her a splendid sunset, with a variety of pinks and oranges mixing on the horizon. She barely had time to enjoy it.

"Damn it! I'm looking for a dead electrician who aspired to be a writer, and I don't know who he is. I'm looking for someone else called *El Oso*, and I'm looking a missing baby who would be twenty-three years old by now, and I don't have a clue what her name is or where she is!"

Chapter 12

Day 10—Wednesday, November 11, 2015

The five o'clock, rush hour traffic heading home from Miami Beach was unbearable. Maria decided to use her time by making several phone calls. Previously she had thought it was dangerous to use her cell while driving, but now that she had Bluetooth in her car and didn't need to hold the phone or even dial the numbers, it was a different matter. First, she called her son and got his voicemail. *He must be in the gym at this hour*, she thought, but just hearing Patrick's voice made her smile. Her father answered on the second ring and not so subtly complained that she had abandoned him.

"No, Papi, we've been working nonstop since the beginning of the week on that terrible case in Homestead."

"I know, I read about it in the papers."

She detected a certain sarcasm in his tone, but she tenderly replied.

"Really, I haven't had a single free minute to call you, and now I'm tied up once again with the case that we reopened."

"And how it's going?"

"I have a few leads, but I'm not close to solving it."

"That's how it goes sometimes, but then suddenly you see everything clearly, one thing leads to another, and when you least expect it you solve the puzzle. If you'd like to run some things by me…"

"Sure, sometimes talking out loud helps me, and you always have a good nose for these things."

"You want to get a bite to eat? I'll treat."

"Thanks, but I'm beat. I'll come by the house tomorrow for sure. I'll give you a call first."

She was about to call the hospital to get an update on Joaquin del Roble when she got a call. It was David. She had spoken to him a couple of times during the past week but neither of them had brought up the night when they had made love. She was glad. She hadn't had time to sort out her emotions. When she answered, there was a certain sweetness in his voice that unsettled her. She wasn't mistaken. After the initial obligatory small talk, David invited her over to his house that evening.

"The kids are away... I can cook us up something."

She hesitated a moment. She preferred to have their dates at her house where she felt more in control of the situation. She began to make up an excuse:

"I'm on the interstate right now, and the traffic's at a standstill. I've had a few days right out of the movies, and I desperately need a shower."

"So then why don't I come by your house, with the food, around seven thirty? Take a shower and get some rest. Don't worry about anything. I'll take care of everything."

He hung up so quickly that she didn't have time to object. Instead of making more phone calls, she put on some music and, even though the traffic didn't get any better, she started to feel the day's tension easing up.

She greeted David at the door with a kiss on the cheek, but as soon as he had placed all the bags of groceries in the kitchen, without saying another word, he embraced her. He caressed her face with his lips and ran his fingers through her hair, and then kissed her passionately. Almost immediately, she felt that tickle of desire between her legs. He stood there, pulled her against him and ran his hands over her body. It was Maria who guided him to the bedroom. They made passionate love. They wound up out of breath and satisfied with their naked bodies intertwined. They remained there for a good while, she resting her head on his chest, both of them half-asleep, listening to their heartbeats and the rhythm of their breathing as it became increasingly slower.

David was the first to speak.

"Dinner must be cold by now."

"Well, we can heat it up…"

Before getting up, David kissed her on the nose. He started to say something, but then he stopped himself. She was glad he did. She didn't want to overthink things, and words—that desire to define one's emotions—many times ruined relationships.

They ate dinner, drank some wine, listened to music, laughed, and talked about a thousand things except for work and themselves. Both of them felt happy and relaxed. She finally looked at her watch.

"I guess I have to get out of here before midnight to keep my carriage from turning into a pumpkin?" David teased her.

Maria walked him to the door. He hugged her again and started kissing her, this time very slowly, with a soft tenderness that reignited that feeling of burning desire. They wound up in bed yet again. This time there wasn't the same intensity, but instead a puzzling feeling of deep sadness as if both were trying to recover something that they had lost a long time ago. When they finished, Maria inexplicably began to cry. He held her head tight against his chest until they both fell asleep.

When she woke up the next morning, David had already left. On her dresser mirror, he had left a piece of paper with a drawing of a smiley face.

Day 11—Thursday, November 12, 2015

Once she arrived at the office, after stopping for her Cuban coffee, Maria started to sense that something in her felt uneasy about the events of the previous night. She had to spend half of the day without anybody talking to her before she felt more at ease.

She was waiting for the right time to talk to Larry and ask him to approve her trip to New York. Meanwhile, she began to go over her report along with her notes. Lazo had come from Cuba when he was seventeen. It was possible that the couple in question had provided him with false documents, perhaps only so that he could pass for eighteen, or maybe in order to hide something that had happened in Cuba. Perhaps they were blackmailing him and that's why they had met in Miami Beach, so that he could pay them. Something had happened to his uncle. Was this couple involved in his death and the baby's disappearance?

She decided to go through the suitcase one more time that Gladys Elena Gonzalez had given her with the belongings of her deceased husband. She put on a pair of gloves and began to place every item on the desk until the suitcase was empty. As she gingerly felt her way along the top, she realized that there was a compartment that she hadn't noticed before. Inside she found a manila envelope. She anxiously opened it and was surprised to find several green sheets of paper in which Lazo was seeking a job at Radio Marti. Then, among the papers, she found another one, a white one that was thicker. It was his fingerprints that had been taken right there in the very same station! Maria couldn't believe it. The document was dated August 21, 1992, the Friday immediately before Hurricane Andrew would batter Florida. Every time they took fingerprints, they always gave one copy to the individual and also kept another on file at the station. She had looked everywhere but hadn't been able to find Lazo's fingerprints and, the entire time, they had been right there, somewhere in that very building! After spending a few hours filling out forms, making calls, and asking for authorization, she finally managed to gain access to the warehouse where they stored old archives. She spent the rest of the afternoon going through a mound of papers that had never been filed due to the hurricane.

Around five in the afternoon, she returned to her desk with two sheets of paper on which were clearly visible the black ink marks of ten fingers belonging to the man whose identity she had been seeking. She was so excited about her discovery that she couldn't wait to knock on Larry's door.

"I found his prints. We have to compare them to the ones at Immigration and send them to Cuba. Also, I'm heading off to New York," she told him without beating around the bush.

She had to explain things in more detail if her boss was going to give her the green light.

Maria felt that indescribable feeling that invaded her every time she came across a new clue.

Chapter 13

Day 11—Thursday, November 12, 2015

The first thing Maria did when she got to the office was compare Lazo's fingerprints with those in the Department of Immigration's database. She didn't find anything. She called a friend who worked there, but she was on vacation. She thought about calling Larrea and asking him to set up a meeting with his writer friend in New York. If he had falsified some documents, he surely wouldn't want to talk to the police, but perhaps if his friend explained the case, it would be easier. She was about to dial the number when Fernandez walked in the office.

"Hey, Fernandez. Do me a favor..." she explained to him what she needed.

"Look, I'll even take you with me to Manhattan if I can...but I'm not promising anything."

Maria left her colleague working on setting up a meeting with the novelist in the Big Apple, and, after calling Gladys Elena and confirming that she was home, she went to Hialeah again.

After the coffee ritual and Maria answering, once again, that she hadn't found Gladys's daughter yet, Maria asked, "Did you know that your husband was looking for a job with Radio Marti?"

"No... Was it an electrician's job?"

"No, as an editor. Was he a writer?"

"He wanted to be. He wrote me some poems, one for our daughter when she was born, and he had published a few things under a pseudonym... He said that they were political in nature and, that if he used his real name, they could've persecuted his family."

"What family did he have in Cuba?"

"Truth is that he never had any contact with them when we were together…he never gave me specific information."

"You didn't suspect anything?"

"No. He was good to me. He was a decent man. I've already told you that."

"Your mother thinks that he was hiding something."

"My mother has a vivid imagination. She barely knew him. She didn't like him because she wanted me to marry my boyfriend from Pinar del Rio and, as you know, in the end that's what happened."

"Did you know a couple, older than he, who were his friends?"

"No."

"Did he ever disappear unexpectedly?"

"No… Why are you asking me this?"

"Please be patient, I'll explain later."

"Did he have money problems?"

"We didn't live lavishly, but we made do."

"Did he get a lot of phone calls that made him nervous?"

"No… Actually, now that you mention it, only once right before the hurricane and the accident. Ray had a beeper. My God, I had forgotten about those things! Now we all have cell phones… Because of his work, they had to be able to reach him at any hour. One time he returned a call, and he said very little. At the time, he said he was going out to get something—I don't know what—and he left. He was gone for more than an hour. I remember because I was giving the baby a bottle, and she took forever to drink it. I was watching an hour-long TV show, and, when it ended, I thought it was odd that he hadn't returned. I'm not the jealous type. I was just worried that something had happened. But he came back a little while later, and he was fine, and in a good mood. Well, a normal one… I had to put the baby to bed, and I didn't bother asking him why he took so long. I think that was a week or so before Hurricane Andrew…"

"Do you have what he wrote?"

"I didn't give them to you before because they're so personal…the poems…and I honestly forgot about them because I didn't put the envelope in the briefcase. But if you want them…"

"I'd like to see them, but if they don't seem useful to the case, I won't take them with me."

Gladys Elena left the little room and came back shortly with a bulging envelope.

Maria looked at the family photos once again and, before opening the envelope, asked Gladys Elena point-blank:

"So there's another thing that intrigues me here. Your daughter Elenita looks a lot like her father, doesn't she?"

"Yes, everyone says that…it's a striking resemblance."

"But Elenita also looks like those drawings of what Gladys Mercedes would look like at this age, right?"

"Yes, certainly."

"So your older daughter also looks like your husband, but he isn't her father. How do you explain that?"

For a moment, the woman appeared thrown but quickly regained her composure.

"I don't know. Resemblances are subjective. When Mauricio and I were young, people thought we were siblings and they'd freak out if they saw us kissing… They said we looked alike… Not so much now, because I don't have black hair like I had back then and we've both put on weight..."

"Did the person who made those drawings of your daughter ever meet Elenita?"

"No, they do it on the computer using a baby picture of her, one of me, and one of her father."

Duquesne sensed that this woman was also hiding something, but she didn't press. She opened the envelope. She read two or three yellowed pages with poems that struck her as mediocre but sincere, and afterwards she flipped through a black and white marbled composition book like the ones used in school. In small but clear writing, there were drafts of articles, poems, phone numbers, and addresses noted in the margins, and some sort of diary.

"Ok, I'll leave the poems with you, but I'd like to take the notebook. I promise that I'll take care of it and give it back to you. Maybe there's a name or a phone number that could give us a lead."

"I've read it many times and I've never found anything, but go ahead and take it. I hope it helps you."

Maria detected some semblance of hostility or uneasiness in the woman's voice. Without a doubt, something had changed between them.

When she got back to the station, Fernandez welcomed her with great enthusiasm. He did everything short of jumping for joy.

"I spoke...I spoke with Bengochea, and he agreed to see us on Saturday because he has work tomorrow. I think it would help if I came along... I've already priced tickets and going one day and coming back the next is expensive, but I can pay mine with miles if there's no budget, and I found a reasonably priced hotel a few blocks from Times Square, and the ticket would cost less if we return on Monday."

Maria had only gone to New York once, with her parents. It was her high school graduation gift. She remembered when they went up to the Empire State Building and took in the amazing view of the city. She even had pictures of the three of them in Rockefeller Center. She was overwhelmed by St. Patrick's Cathedral where her mother had lit many candles, but the best part was seeing *Cats* on Broadway. The song "Memory" greatly moved her parents. She didn't understand back then why Cubans wore their emotions on their sleeve. Now these images of her happy, youthful mother invoked a bittersweet sensation, and Maria understood better the pain of life's losses.

Chapter 14

Days 12 and 13—Friday and Saturday, November 13 and 14, 2015

They bought tickets for a flight that would leave Miami on Friday evening at quarter to six and arrive at LaGuardia around nine. That way they could get in a full day of work and arrive in New York early that night. They arranged a breakfast meeting with Bengochea for nine thirty the next morning.

Maria had to find something in her closet that would be appropriate for the New York fall temperatures. Everything she tried on was out of style. She thought it was silly to spend money on clothes she would never wear in Miami, but early that morning she ran over to Dolphin Mall and bought herself a leather jacket and a black sweater from Burlington Coat Factory, getting good deals on both. It didn't take her long to pack for a two-day trip. She called her father and asked him to take her to the airport. That way they could visit on the way. She texted Patrick because she knew that was the best way to get in touch with him. She wondered if she should call David. She opted to write to him instead, saying that she was going to New York for the weekend for an interview related to the case. Actually, it was unnecessary because anyone with a cell phone could reach her as easily in Miami as in Timbuktu.

She didn't know how Fernandez had managed to get them such a reasonable rate in the Millennium Broadway Hotel in the heart of Times Square. It was an older hotel with lots of white veined brownish marble, displaying the splendor of a different era, and looked a little dated. The rooms, however, met all modern standards. She had barely hung up the four outfits she brought when Fernandez, who was staying two floors above, knocked on the door asking if she was ready to go. Maria was surprised by the natural way her colleague could flow amidst the comings and goings of such a diverse population, the brilliant neon lights, and the never-ending traffic dominated by yellow taxis. She was a little uneasy, but two streets later, she felt a great rush like when she went to the Miami-Dade County Youth Fair as a child and rode the roller coaster with her friends. Fernandez took her by the hand, and they went into a crowded bar where it was so loud you couldn't hear your own thoughts.

"We'll have a beer here and later we'll grab some Cuban-Chinese food."

Two beers and twenty minutes later, Maria was feeling so great that it was hard to leave. She didn't regret it. Although they had to walk a few blocks to get to the Calle Dao restaurant, it was worth it. Maria didn't know what to choose from such an extensive and surprising menu. Duck empanadas? Roasted pork with fried rice?

Fernandez, on the other hand, was looking at the right side of the menu and said, somewhat embarrassed, "These prices aren't like the ones at the Chinese-Cuban joints my parents used to take me to."

Maria assured him they would split the check.

They ate heartily. The place was full, but not packed, and one of the waiters explained to them that during lunch and happy hour they had a hard time fitting everyone in, and that the regulars were people who worked nearby. The restaurant had been open little more than a year and was already a great success.

Maria thought about looking over the questions she and Fernandez would ask Bengochea the next day, but, when they got back to the hotel, she was so exhausted that she chose to just go to bed and meet back up with him in the lobby at eight in the morning.

The writer told them to meet in a café close to where he lived in Brooklyn. She preferred to take a cab. She really wanted to go over the famous bridge, but Fernandez insisted they take the subway. The station was very close by, and they got off five stops later at Prospect Park. Maria was surprised by the massive park where the fall colors were at peak. She couldn't help herself, and she took out her phone and snapped pictures of the red, brown, and golden leaves. Meanwhile, Fernandez was punching in the address of their destination in his phone's GPS.

"Ok, it's in Park Slope, in one of the nearby neighborhoods. The houses are on the streets, which run east to west, and businesses line the avenues."

They didn't have any difficulty finding Roots Café on 5th Avenue, a wide two-way thoroughfare with cars parked at meters along both sides and several two and three-story buildings that housed travel agencies, insurance companies, health food stores, fruit markets, and a few restaurants. Roots Café was in the basement of a red brick building. On the walls hung a number of guitars and a cheap painting of a matador about to kill a bull. The menu was posted in big letters behind the counter. There weren't more than seven or eight tables. She saw a man with a navy blue sweater and a laptop sitting at one of the tables. She immediately knew it was Bengochea and went over to greet him.

He was surprised.

"I wasn't expecting a female officer…much less such a pretty one."

In general, this type of comment, which she had heard before, irritated her, and what made it even worse was when he looked her up and down, visually undressing her. Nonetheless, to her surprise, she felt pleased; it was nice to know that she could still attract a man.

Fernandez sensed the brief moment of tension between the two and rushed to introduce himself, but Bengochea hardly looked at him. He treated him more like he was his employee.

"Why don't you order breakfast for the three of us? The special is really good here… In the meantime, Duquesne and I will get to know each other a little better."

Maria, maybe without realizing it, did the same thing the writer did moments before. She looked at his balding head, with only a few white hairs on the sides, his gray beard, short and well groomed, and his full gray mustache and eyebrows that arched over eyes as dark as the bottom of a well. His body was muscular, hard. *He looks like Sean Connery,* she thought. She noticed he wore a wedding ring and remembered her mother's advice: *Never get involved with a married man. It will never end well.* Why had she remembered that? Could it be that she was actually attracted to this stranger? Why were these long-lost sensations coming back to her?

"Well then…how can I help you? By the way, we're speaking informally, right? It's always like that among Cubans. And, you are both Cuban, aren't you?"

"Fernandez was born in Cuba, but came when he was young. I was born here. I guess you could say we're Cuban Americans."

"Ah! We'll I've spent thirty-five years in the United States and I'm still Cuban…"

"I get that."

"Many who came through Mariel don't want to know anything about Cuba, or at least that's what they say, but…"

At that moment Fernandez came back with a tray of three steaming cups of coffee and some egg, cheese, and sausage sandwiches that looked delicious. They ate in silence for a few minutes. It was Fernandez who broke the ice.

"I've read just about all of your work. The book about the training camps in Matanzas really moved me. It's so realistic that it almost seems like you witnessed it firsthand, and the Major's character is really well defined—a decent man who feels like he has to act against his principles in order to survive…which still happens in Cuba."

Bengochea choked on his sandwich. Maria realized that Fernandez's comment wasn't unwarranted, and she was grateful that he had come with her. She broke into the conversation.

"So then, we aren't trying to find out what you might have done in Cuba… We're trying to solve a case of a man who died in an accident when his car fell into a canal in Miami in 1992, and now it looks like he was murdered. We suspect that a couple helped him falsify documents and then blackmailed him later. They might have had something to do with his death. Since you were in the Orange Bowl and Tamiami Park maybe you'll remember them. We believe that people called him *El Oso*."

Bengochea regained his color. He continued eating slowly. Maria realized that he was thinking about his answer.

"Yes, I met them, but it's been a long time since I've heard anything about them. Plus, I think they're dead. At least he is…that's the rumor that went around a few years ago."

Maria couldn't believe what she just heard. She knew that if she could have found the couple, they could get to the bottom of it.

"What can you tell me about them?"

"Well, I don't know where they learned it, but they were masters of falsifying documents. They could make a transcript from the University of Havana just as easily as a birth certificate from some village on the Island, a passport, and even a social security card with a dead man's number. He was a cynic. He said coarsely that the only thing he didn't falsify was cash… I didn't know if she was with him out of love or fear. She seemed like the better person. What I mean is, she spoke with less arrogance and was polite, but she was an accomplice all the same."

"Do you know their names, where they might have lived?"

"All he went by was *El Oso*. Now that I think about it, maybe because he had so much hair on his chest and arms… He always wore a partially unbuttoned shirt with a big chain and medallion of Saint Barbara, I think, or I don't know, maybe Our Lady of Charity, or Saint Lazarus… I don't remember her name, although the face is coming back to me… She had one of those really Spanish names…Dolores, Milagros, Fe… Soledad… That's it, her name was Soledad. I'm sure because that was one of my paternal aunt's names."

"If I get a police sketch artist, would you be willing to work with him to make a pencil rendition of their faces and also look at some photos to see if you recognize them?"

Bengochea looked uncomfortable. Once again, Fernandez chimed in smoothly.

"We know how busy you are. I know that you're about to finish a new novel, but we won't take up much of your time. We'll try to have everything all ready by the time you get to the station. It'll only take a few minutes, and we'll arrange a taxi for you if that's better, preferably this afternoon because we're heading back to Miami on Monday."

Bengochea looked at him condescendingly...

"I don't think I can today... I have a conflict tonight. You do know that in this very spot on Saturdays poets and singers have a pretty eclectic gathering? Maybe you guys would like to come..."

"Me? Of course. What time?" Fernandez asked.

"It starts at eight o'clock but doesn't get going until around ten."

"Then we'll arrange your visit at the station for two or four o'clock in the afternoon; you'll have ample time."

Bengochea laughed in such an exaggerated fashion that his abdominal muscles moved.

"Wow, man, you're worse than Duquesne... You're persistent."

"I'd really appreciate it," Maria said in her sweetest and most seductive tone.

"Fine, set it up and let me know."

As they said goodbye, Fernandez started looking for information on his phone.

"Check this out Maria, the 78th Precinct is the closest, but the 68th is also in Brooklyn, and, even though it's a little farther away, it's considered one of the best in the country. I'd go there."

"Ok, but we're going to call Larry to touch base first."

Some twenty minutes later, the taxi stopped in front of a huge, gray and blue cement building.

The call with Larry had been productive. They helped them right away and assured them that an artist would be available to do the sketches at two thirty in the afternoon. The photo issue was more complicated. They didn't really know where Soledad lived nor whether she even had a criminal record. The sergeant suggested that after they had the sketch done they could take a picture and see if the database recognized the facial features.

When they left the office in the afternoon with Bengochea and the drawings of both *El Oso* and his partner in crime, Maria was euphoric. She felt like she was close to tying up all the loose ends.

Chapter 15

Day 15—Monday, November 16, 2015

Maria didn't wait to return to Miami before getting back at it. Her office had informed her that she had a message from Joaquin del Roble who had returned to The Palace and wanted to see her. While still in La Guardia she made an appointment for four thirty in the afternoon, since she knew that Lazo's uncle would take a siesta until four. She stopped by the house to drop off her suitcase, look at the mail, and touch up her hair and makeup. She was at the office just long enough to find her notes on the interview with Don Joaquin. She was in the luxurious lobby right on time, but this time the exiled Spaniard wasn't waiting for her there. They explained that he was in a different building for the time being because he needed additional care.

Once she saw him, Maria had to mask her sadness. In just a few days, he had seemed to age. Only the deep blue eyes reminded her of the elegant and learned gentleman that she had met at the beginning of the investigation. He was seated in an overstuffed armchair, in pajamas, and wearing an elegant robe. He had a blanket over his legs.

"I don't know why I'm always cold," he said after greeting her, as if he had realized that she thought it was odd to see him so bundled up on a sunny, warm day.

"After all these years I'm still not used to air conditioning," he insisted. "But please, Miss, have a seat…"

Maria asked him about his health. Don Joaquin made a gesture with his hand like he was shooing away flies.

"So-so, that's why it was so urgent that I see you. I'm fine, don't make that face, but one never knows."

"Don't talk like that…"

"Don't worry. Nobody is going to miss me… But let's not talk about me."

"Whatever you say."

Maria took out her recorder and notepad, and he gave his consent with a nod of the head.

"By the way, I didn't tell you the end of the story about my relationship with Alberto… He had been working and living with me for about ten years. He wasn't a kid anymore but a man. He was reserved, but nice and appreciative…or so I thought for many years. He did his job. He helped around the yard and fixed whatever broke in the house. He was very handy. He was very resourceful. He'd use a hanger when someone else would have gone to Home Depot in search of some tool. He told me that in Cuba he had learned to make do with what he had. He would call his mother now and then. He always asked permission and insisted on paying for the call. One time he put me on the phone with her, and although I'm really not very sentimental, I was moved by how kindly she spoke about my brother. She even said that her mother, before she died, recognized that Juancho had been the love of her life. You see, I always thought that my brother had never had a woman who loved him."

"What else did Alberto or his mother tell you about life in Cuba? Did she live in Havana or Matanzas?"

"In Havana… I think in an apartment in La Vibora…you know, the neighborhood… Santa Catalina is the main street with real mansions, but the side streets have more modest homes and buildings. I knew Havana really well because we would deliver all the hats my mother made for her clients."

"Alberto didn't say anything to you about Matanzas?"

"No, if he was born there, he left as a young child because all of his stories were about Havana…except for when he went off to the countryside as part of his schooling. You know how Cuba was back then. I don't think it's like that anymore."

"Did your nephew have friends in Miami?"

"Very few. Sometimes he would go out for a beer with his friends from work. I never went along. They were my employees, and it didn't feel right to me."

"Did he have a girlfriend or was there a special woman?"

"There was one who used to drive a FedEx truck—you know how things have changed—and she'd deliver the parts we ordered. Sometimes I saw them talking and you know...flirting. But Alberto was reserved, kind of quiet...it didn't make any difference to me. I like to read, listen to music, and, since I was used to being alone, I wasn't a big talker, either. All things considered, I found his company pleasant."

"So what happened?"

"Well, look, I don't know. Around 1990 he started getting very restless. He'd speak mysteriously on the phone. He'd go out at all hours. He asked me if he could work extra hours to make more. Then he told me very delicately that he was very grateful, but he wanted to move out and live alone. I thought he might have a woman and that's who he was talking to and going to see, and that's why he needed more privacy. It made me sad that he was moving, but I understood. We remained good friends, and he kept doing great at work. He would still come to the house to cut my grass, and he always refused to charge me."

Don Joaquin paused and took a drink of water.

"I prefer wine or whiskey at this hour, but they won't let me have it."

Maria knew that he needed the break in order to continue, and she suspected that he was about to reveal something important to her.

"Look, Miss, you can see what happened next in the police reports. Two masked men broke into my shop very early in the morning, at the only hour I was alone. They held me up at gunpoint and made me go to the safe. They knew where it was, right behind a bookcase. I didn't have any other option than to open it. They took off with about forty thousand dollars because a customer had paid in cash the day before, and I was waiting for one of the security guards I sometimes use to accompany me to the bank the next morning. I'm sure someone tipped them off…"

"And did you suspect Alberto?"

"Not at the beginning. The truth is I didn't know who to suspect. All my employees had been with me for years, and I had never had any problems. If I suspected anyone, it would have been a girl, Magda, not because she was a bad person, just a little ditsy and indiscreet. She had just gone through a divorce, and I thought that maybe she had a boyfriend and that, maybe without realizing it, she had told him things. The police investigated but they never caught the thieves, and I never got the money back except for what the insurance covered… But the story doesn't end there."

Once again, Don Joaquin took a sip of water before continuing.

"A few months later, they came into my house despite the alarms—they must have known how good they were. They knew exactly how to disable them and where I kept the safe. This time they didn't get hardly any money, but they did take some jewelry that had belonged to my mother and some that was Antonia's. Nothing of great monetary value, just sentimental. It seems that it made them mad that there hadn't been more, so before leaving they beat me up pretty bad. I lost consciousness and wasn't able to call the police until many hours later. This time they recovered my mother's wedding band in a pawnshop, but that was all… and the case is still unresolved. The police aren't always very efficient."

"Before there were fewer resources then than now," Maria defended herself.

"I know, Miss, I'm kidding. It doesn't matter."

"And did you suspect Alberto?"

"Well, you're going to think I'm stupid but at the beginning, no. Or maybe I didn't want to because I knew perfectly well that he was the only one who knew my house well."

"What happened next?"

"At first, little things. Don't laugh. I realized that he wouldn't look me in the eye, that he would get nervous each time he looked at me, even that he had lost weight and sweated a lot. I thought that maybe he felt guilty and that I should confront him to see if he'd tell me the truth. The police advised me not to do it, but the situation had me very uneasy."

"Did you ever speak to him?"

"Not really. One Friday he got paid and, before leaving, he put an envelope on my desk. He thanked me for everything I had done for him, and he told me that he was quitting his job and that he was leaving Miami. I didn't hear anything else about him until almost two years later."

Don Joaquin looked at the clock that showed six thirty. A girl came in with some medicines and a dinner tray.

"You can come back tomorrow if you would like…"

Maria understood that she would have to wait until the next visit to hear the end of the story. But Don Joaquin had already given her important clues. Lazo had gotten involved in criminal activity—either voluntarily or by blackmail—or, at a minimum, he provided information to facilitate it. Even though she seemed to understand better the man whose death she was investigating, she was still missing many pieces of the puzzle. Most of all, knowing whether the little baby that was traveling with him in the car was still alive and where to find her.

Chapter 16

Day 16—Tuesday, November 17, 2015

The ringer on her cell woke her up at four in the morning. Patrick was speaking quickly and she was so sound asleep that it took a few minutes to figure out what he was telling her. One of his friends from the University of Florida had fallen from the sixth floor, and the ambulance had taken him unconscious and bloodied.

"Mami, I wasn't with him because I have an exam tomorrow and I don't like to go out during the week... Maybe if I had gone, this wouldn't have happened to him..."

"Patrick, you can't think like that. You can't take care of everybody."

"Mami, I don't know what could've happened. He's my age, he plays hockey, and he gets good grades. He's nice, a good friend... He isn't a drinker and doesn't do drugs..."

"Hopefully he has only broken a few bones and will recover."

"I don't know... When I got there, they had already taken him away and the place where he fell was surrounded by yellow tape, and there was so much blood!"

Patrick hung up when he got to the hospital where they had taken his friend, and he promised to call her when he knew something. Maria didn't even bother going back to sleep. She fixed herself a cup of tea and got comfortable in her armchair with a blanket on her lap along with her cell phone. Not even ten minutes had gone by when Patrick called again. This time it was even harder to understand him because he was sobbing. As a mother, she never remembered him crying like that. He kept repeating:

"He died. Mami, he died… Why? Why? He was twenty years old, just like me."

Maria tried to comfort him, telling him that there were things that couldn't be explained, that it was hard to face the death of a person your own age…but her words sounded empty even to her, so she had to make a strong effort to stay calm. A different and terrible question kept pounding in her head: what if it had been Patrick?

"Mami, I met him back in Miami…he's from Weston…his family came from Venezuela fleeing the violence there because Henry was involved in student protests…and look…coming here and dying!"

"*Mijo*, do you want me to call your father or grandfather, or would you like to come home for a few days?"

"I can't right now, Mami. I'm in the middle of exams…and work. It'll be Thanksgiving soon, and I'll come then."

"Ok, *Mijo*, but stay calm…take care of yourself…call me whenever you want to…"

Maria decided to wait until seven o'clock to call Bill. It surprised her that Patrick had already told him everything, and she could say that her ex-husband was actually nice to her.

"You more than anybody see the problems that are out there today… Sometimes I wonder if we did the right thing letting him go to Gainesville…but there's danger everywhere and I think that living alone has made him grow up."

"Yesterday he was crying like a baby."

"Not so much with me. You know that crying doesn't look manly. Patrick went through his grandmother's death, but he had never experienced the death of someone his own age. Only when he was in daycare and that child shot himself playing with his father's gun. Do you remember?"

"Of course I remember. We prayed for Tim for almost three months before Patrick finally accepted that by then he had probably gotten to Heaven."

They laughed. It was the first time that they remembered their son's childhood together and found a topic of conversation that didn't result in a fight. Maria was glad because that morning she had understood that the boy needed them both.

Patrick had also called his grandfather.

"I offered to go up there, but he told me it wasn't necessary, that he had to study…so I'll stay with my plan to go python hunting."

The increase of those invasive reptiles was threatening the indigenous fauna of the Everglades' delicate ecosystem. Two years ago, they had created a program to enlist volunteers to hunt snakes that could be up to twenty-six feet long. When it was cold, they would come out on the highways to sun and that's when it was easiest to catch them. The temperature had recently dipped down a lot for early November. Pythons are not venomous, but they have sharp teeth, and Maria, like her mother, was more afraid of reptiles than the fiercest lions.

"Oh, Papi, I don't know why you get involved with those things… Be careful, please…"

"*Mija*, I have to have something to amuse myself…"

"If Mami were alive she wouldn't let you."

"I wouldn't have dared ask!" answered the old policeman with a smile that didn't hide the longing for his companion of so many years.

"Look, Maria, one more thing…"

When her father called her Maria, it was always something serious.

"Maybe you can find out something about Patrick's friend who died. What he told me sounds odd. A twenty-year-old falling from a balcony?

Maybe they put something in his drink… I know that the police are investigating it… You have lots of friends in so many places…"

She realized that her father was just as worried about Patrick as she was.

"I'll see what I can find out…and I hope that you don't catch any snakes!"

"Well, honey, if it's for the good of Mother Earth…"

Once back in the office, Maria called Elaine, her contact in the Immigration Department. She confirmed what Maria suspected. The fingerprints that she had found for Lazo matched those of Alberto Gonzalez who had been in Tamiami Park in 1980 and had entered the country at the age of seventeen. But there wasn't anything else on him. It was as if the earth had swallowed him up.

With those facts, she went to see her boss to suggest that they send the prints to Cuba.

Larry had her come in and sit down as soon as her knuckles touched the door. He didn't let her speak.

"I'm glad you've come in. I was just about to call you. We've gotten a response from the Cuban government. They suggest that you go there, and they say they'll collaborate however they can."

Maria moved uncomfortably in the chair. She had always wanted to get to know the mythic land of her parents. But she didn't know if she was ready and whether she wanted to return in that way, on the job.

"Look, they say that you should get in touch with this policeman who will be the one to work with you."

When he handed her the paper, she didn't know if it was a joke.

"Boss, there's no way. How is it possible that I'm supposed to work with Mario Conde? He's a literary character in Leonardo Padura's novels. I've read them all."

"Maria, what do I know… maybe the character is based on a real person…"

"He isn't going to use the same name…"

"Well maybe he's called that because of the character, or it's a coincidence. Who knows?"

"Look, Larry, I was coming to tell you that we've confirmed that the fingerprints match a certain Alberto Gonzalez who came through Mariel and said that he was seventeen, which was possibly true, although later in the papers it looked like he'd been born two years earlier. How about we send the prints to see if they can give us any information before deciding if I should go… It's a huge expense."

Larry knew that Maria's doubts didn't have anything to do with the budget, but he agreed to send the prints before they decided about her trip.

"It's just that you've been on this case for two weeks now, and I'd like for us to resolve it soon."

"You and me both. Believe me."

Chapter 17

Day 17—Wednesday, November 18, 2015

Maria was awakened by the cell phone swoosh announcing she had a message. Lourdes wanted her to call her back. She saw that it was 6:50 a.m., the hour when her alarm would have rung. She turned it off, washed her face, and called her mother's friend, who began to speak hurriedly.

"Oh, Mariita, this time he really left me… He packed his suitcase, told me that he had thought a lot about me and the children before making the decision, that I would hear from him later, and he left…"

"Without giving you an explanation?"

"Nothing, all he said was that soon I would hear from him. I suppose he must be talking about divorce papers. Imagine, more than fifty years of marriage!"

Lourdes was sobbing.

"Look, sweetie, there has to be another reason."

Maria was trying to lift her spirits, but when she remembered that she had seen him with a young woman in Hialeah, she didn't know what to think.

"But what else could have made him pack a bag and leave?"

"Let's see, was it a large suitcase? What did he take?"

"No, it was a carry-on, and he packed two changes of clothing, pajamas, a shaving kit…a toothbrush…those things…"

"Anything else? Think."

"Well, one weird thing, when he was at the door he returned to the office and grabbed a family photo that he had on his desk, and I think a small Cuban flag, too."

"Lourdes, those aren't things that a man takes when he's about to leave his wife. Did he tell you where he was going?"

"No, but I'm almost sure that he had an airplane ticket…"

"Did he take his passport?"

"I don't know…let me check."

Lourdes had calmed down a little, and, while she waited, Maria made coffee. This morning she wasn't able to hold out for her typical morning shot of coffee at the kiosk.

"The passport is here," Lourdes said in a certain happy tone for the first time in the entire conversation.

"Lourdes, I assure you that it isn't what you think. It's probably a business trip…or one of those crazy political things that he gets into… Let me see if I can find out anything. And you promise me that you'll calm down and let me know if anything changes."

"Do you think that I should tell the kids?"

Maria answered her with a question:

"Why would you worry them and make them doubt their father? Later on, when it turns out to be nothing, you'll regret it."

"Alright…if you think so…"

"I'll call you later to see how you are," Duquesne promised her.

As soon as she arrived at the station, Fernandez greeted her with great excitement.

"We've had several calls from people who saw the sketches of the counterfeiters! I was waiting so that you could tell me whether you wanted to answer them yourself or if we should split the work..."

Maria was surprised because there were ten messages from various parts of the country. She took the five that were from Miami and the New York area and gave the rest to Fernandez.

"Ok, let's begin. If you find out anything unusual, tell me, and I'll do the same and we can compare notes in a few hours. Does that sound like a plan?"

Fernandez was happy to collaborate on the case.

The two first calls that Maria made were answered by voicemail, and she left messages. The third was to a woman in Miami that had arrived through Mariel and swore she had seen the couple in Tamiami Park.

"Here's the thing, they approached me and told me they could get me out of there in a few hours, but when I saw that the papers were fake, I turned it down. I've always been a law-abiding person and if I told lies to be able to leave Cuba, it was for extenuating circumstances, but I was not going to keep on with the lies. That always ends badly."

"Are you sure it was them?"

"Absolutely...they spent all their time circulating around the place."

"Do you know of anybody who may have accepted their services?"

"Lots of people, but I don't remember names. I never saw any of them ever again."

"And have you heard anything else about them?"

"No...I heard rumors that later they went to *For Chafi*, is that how you say it?"

"You mean Fort Chaffee in Arkansas?"

"Yes, where they took lots of refugees…but I don't know if it's true. Then they told me that they'd had a daughter…but I can't say that for sure either. I never saw them again."

Maria's heart fluttered. It was the first time that someone had mentioned the girl. She was more and more convinced that the couple had killed Lazo and kidnaped the baby girl, but why? And where was that girl who must be older than twenty-three now?

She asked the woman to call her back if she remembered anything else and jotted down in very large letters her name, phone number, and the information she had provided.

Before that, she sent an email to her friend Aldo del Pozo who had worked for a few months in Fort Chaffee, sending him the sketches and asking him whether he had recalled the couple. She immediately received an autoreply that he was on a trip. She would have to wait a few more days.

They must have written down the wrong number on the fourth call to New York because they got a recording that it had been disconnected. She asked the operator to verify the number of a call that had come in at 9:06 a.m. Sure enough, the last two numbers were inverted. When she finally got through, a man identifying himself as Pedro Gonzalez answered. He told her that he had arrived from Cuba in the sixties and, to her surprise, he said terrible things about Jacinto Bengochea, and he assured her that the couple had falsified documents for him. When Maria tried to get him to give more information about himself and details about the accusations against Bengochea, the man swore he didn't know anything else and hung up. *The most likely thing is that this diatribe against the successful Marielito writer stemmed from envy,* thought the detective, and she decided that she would only look deeper if the accusations came up again.

The last call was to New Jersey. She spoke with Odalys Fuentes, an elderly woman who assured her that *El Oso* had died in an accident and that for a short time she had taken care of Sole when she was four or five, but then later Soledad and the child had left the area and she had never heard from them again.

"As much as I loved that child, and they didn't even send me a postcard, or an address, or even a phone number! It was as if the earth swallowed them."

Once again, Maria felt her heart speed up. She was sure that "Sole" was the missing child. The mother obviously lived on the run. She asked the woman whether she had any pictures of the child.

"Maybe one or two, but not many because with her being so beautiful, her mother didn't like her to be photographed. One time she grabbed the camera out of my hands. Later she apologized and told me a bizarre story about how her little cousin had her portrait made when she was young and it brought her bad luck, but I think there was more to it."

Since Odalys didn't have email, Maria couldn't send her any of the sketches that showed how the girl would look at different ages, but she took her name and address and agreed to send it by express mail.

"As soon as you receive it, please call me, and also if you find any pictures. It is extremely important."

Even though she promised her, Maria felt like something was bothering the woman and did not want to hang up just yet. And, indeed, that was the case. When Maria asked if there was a problem, she said:

"Look, it's probably best not to send it by express mail because sometimes they knock on the door, I'm a little deaf, I don't hear well, and they hold it for me to pick up. The post office is far away and…"

Maria calmed her down:

"Don't worry. I will mail it to you today through regular mail."

Before going back to the earlier calls, she saw that Fernandez was coming toward her grinning from ear to ear.

"Maria, a teacher in Tampa had Soledad as a high school student. She recognized the mother."

Detective Duquesne told her colleague what she had found out. She knew that the clues were getting them closer to solving the mystery. Fernandez suggested that they celebrate by going to lunch at a nice restaurant, but Maria preferred to drop by her father's house.

As always, the old man was happy to see her when she arrived with two *medianoches*, a flan to share, and a Cuban coffee.

"I'll pour us a beer..."

She was going to respond that she preferred not to drink when she was working, but an image on TV caught her attention.

"Turn up the volume, Papi, please."

She managed to hear that a group of Cubans had declared a hunger strike in front of the New York Times protesting a series of articles against the embargo and in favor of renewing diplomatic relations between Cuba and the United States. Standing in the middle of the crowd, she could clearly make out Lourdes's husband. She was about to call her when her cell rang. It was Lourdes:

"Did you see? On a hunger strike in New York! Why didn't he tell me anything? I wouldn't have allowed it!"

"Well, that's exactly why he didn't tell you, Lourdita," Maria answered with a chuckle.

Chapter 18

Days 18–21—Thursday through Sunday, November 19 through 22, 2015

Maria doubted whether she should go see Gladys Elena Lazo and bring her up to date on the new developments on her daughter. During the last conversation that they had, she perceived that the woman was holding something back from her, and she was interested in seeing her again, but, at the same time, she didn't want to give her false hopes. She was going back and forth on whether she should touch base with her or finish making the remaining calls when they informed her that Mercy had come to see her. She'd hardly had time to tell them to send her in when a whirlwind of a woman was standing right in front of her:

"Look, Duchess, my granddaughter's alive. Now I know it for sure. You have to find her."

"Take a seat, ma'am, please."

But the woman preferred to stand, very shaken, talking with her hands, and speaking wildly.

Maria tried to calm her down:

"Look, Mercy, if you don't speak to me slowly and tell me what's happened, it won't help us solve the case."

"This is much more than a case! What you need to do is find my granddaughter who I know is still alive."

"Have you seen her?"

"Yes…well, no…"

"What do you mean 'yes, well, no'?"

"I haven't seen her in person, just in dreams…but believe me, this has happened to me before… I haven't talked about it with other people, but I knew that my husband was going to drown on that raft and that's why I didn't get on it… I saw it in a dream I had the night they left…"

"And now?"

"Look, you know how dreams are. Sometimes they don't make sense… I saw my two granddaughters, Gladys Mercedes and Elenita. They looked so much alike that at first I thought both were Elena, one as a child and another a little older, so it was like, I don't know, seeing her in the past and the future at the same time. But no, it was my older granddaughter, and she didn't have her hair in a bob like the sketches portray her; instead it was very long, and she was wearing a cap and gown, as if it were her graduation…"

Maria began to pay more attention.

"Did you recognize the place?"

"No, I don't know…it wasn't in Miami…the lighting was different… there were other flowers that don't grow here, and the buildings were made of brick…but not red, instead like gray…"

"Did they say anything in the dream?"

"The sisters were talking, but I couldn't hear what they were saying. Without a doubt, the two of them seemed very happy and at the end they hugged one another. And there were a lot of people in the place, and lots of noise, but I don't know what they were talking about. It was like they were celebrating."

"And was there anyone else in the dream?"

"I didn't see anyone else that I knew, but I sensed that the rest of our family was there but we weren't. I can't explain it…"

"Anything else?"

"Yes, I sensed a shadow near Gladysita, very strange, like good and bad at the same time."

"Hmm."

"Do you believe me?"

"I believe that you had a dream, but we have to keep investigating to figure out what it means."

"But do you believe that my granddaughter is alive?"

Maria hesitated but the anguish on the grandmother's face made her decide:

"Yes, Mercy, I too believe that your granddaughter is alive, but you have to let me do my job to find her. I assure you that we're doing everything possible."

She had just returned from accompanying Mercedes to the door and asking her to stay calm when her cell rang.

"Oh, *Mariita*, you have to do something, I'm afraid that Ramon is going to die."

"Lourdes, he hasn't even been on strike for twenty-four hours. Nothing's going to happen to him."

"I don't know, I see him going downhill..."

"That's probably because he hasn't shaved. Let's see, is he drinking water?"

"I think so, it looks like they're drinking water and there's a doctor that goes to see them twice a day. But he's the oldest one in the group! He's crazy... What are they going to gain by this?"

"Lourdes, I don't think he's accomplishing anything, but he sees it differently. He's someone who has never been able to accept what happened in Cuba. Opposing the Revolution is his reason for living."

"But what about me and the kids?"

"I didn't mean to imply that… There are many people in Miami just like him."

"Your father isn't like that…"

"Well, there are all kinds… What do the kids say?"

"Nothing, just that it's one more of their father's crazy things, that the strike will end and nothing will happen."

"Well, they're right."

"Do you think I should go there?"

"What for, Lourdes? I don't see you prepared to support him. I think you shouldn't humiliate him and…"

"Ok, I'll wait and see what happens, but if I think for even one minute that his health is at risk, I swear to you that I'll be on the first flight to New York!"

Just as she hung up, she looked for Fernandez to compare notes and to continue with the calls, but the conversation didn't last long because the chief called all of the police officers to an urgent meeting in the conference room.

Lawrence Keppler informed them with a solemn face that a blood-stained boat had been found washed up on the shore of Biscayne Bay, and the Coast Guard and the Miami Police were requesting that all divisions assist in the search for a missing man.

He freed up two officers who were working on an urgent case to catch a man who had masturbated in front of a few homes early in the mornings and who had tried to sexually assault a young girl as she returned home. Luckily, the girl had resisted and was able to escape. He assigned various tasks to the others. He looked at Duquesne as if he were apologizing that she would have to take a break in her case, and he left another officer and Fernandez in the station to handle any emergencies so that the rest of them could look into the alleged missing man, Richard Kron, who was forty-five. Before leaving, Fernandez and Duquesne exchanged an intuitive look. She knew that he would find the time to keep making calls on the case they were working on together and that they were finally getting some solid clues.

The three days that followed were intense. Maria went to the gym often and kept herself in good shape, but being on a boat or in a helicopter and spending hours with binoculars looking at the immense ocean searching for a body or a survivor was a much more exhausting job than she could have imagined.

On the second day, they found out that the alleged missing person was facing legal charges for money laundering and other crimes. They feared that he might have created a false scenario so that they would presume him dead and he would flee, but it was also possible that they had killed him. They continued the search. On the fourth day, they arrested Kron in a motel in Louisiana on his way to the Mexican border. They had spent about a half million dollars on the investigation because of the fugitive's little stunt. Maria regretted even more having lost four days of work on her case.

It was already three o'clock in the afternoon when they closed the case, thanked all the officers for their help, and dismissed them. When Maria got home, she was so tired that she fell asleep without listening to messages or checking the mail.

Chapter 19

Day 22—Monday, November 23, 2015

She woke up startled, as if she were going to be late somewhere. The clock showed four o'clock in the morning. She had slept for almost twelve hours and knew that she would never fall back asleep. She listened to her voicemails on both her cellphone and landline. The first one was from her father telling her that he had seen her on TV in a helicopter and that she could have given him a heads up; David was aware of her mission, he wished her luck, and asked her to give him a call him when she could; Lourdes announced she was going to New York; Patrick was going to get in on Wednesday for Thanksgiving but needed to leave early Saturday because there was an important football game back at school, and he asked if he could bring a friend. Maria glanced at the calendar. Thanksgiving was this coming Thursday, four days away. Where would she find the time to buy and cook a turkey? She would have to order it. She was looking forward to seeing her son, but she was anxious to focus on finishing the case. Of course, if Patrick came with a friend, he would take up less of her time… *How could I possibly think such a thing, especially with how much I've been missing him? On the other hand, if my son were the one who had disappeared, wouldn't I want a detective who was wholeheartedly devoted to finding him?* All these thoughts were swimming in her head while she waited for her black coffee to finish brewing. She would drink it on the way to the office. She realized she was hungry and poured herself a bowl of cereal only to discover that the milk was sour. She ended up eating an energy bar with her coffee.

She opened her laptop and looked through her email. Most of them were unimportant except for three. The first one was from Dr. John Erwin who told her that they had the results of Lazo's DNA tests; another from Aldo del Pozo, who told her that he wasn't sure if he remembered the couple but would circulate the sketches around to other people; and the last one, a concise, mysterious, and encouraging message from Fernandez—"Good leads. Call when you can."

She showered and got dressed even though it was still too early to go into the office or call anyone. She picked up the paper as soon as she heard it land in the front yard. On the front page was a picture of some Cubans in New York who had ended their hunger strike seemingly at the request of some dissidents that claimed they needed them for "the cause." In the photo, Lourdes appeared smiling and satisfied with Ramon's arm around her. *That didn't last long!* Maria thought to herself sadly. She sympathized with men like Ramon Morales. They were still stuck in the psychological trauma that the Revolution had caused them. Their pain was genuine and along the way, their lives had passed them by.

She felt her phone vibrate with a text message. It was David asking her to call if she was up. It was six thirty. She did so immediately and without even thinking. She had been disconnected from all her loved ones, and it made her happy to talk to people she cared about.

After asking about the failed rescue attempt in the bay, David told her the real reason for his call.

"Listen, the boys are going to be with me for Thanksgiving, and I thought it would be great if your dad, your son, and you could come over too… The three of us are going to cook, and I can't guarantee how it'll turn out, but…"

"Patrick's coming with a friend."

"No problem, where there's enough food for six, there's enough for seven. I've already bought a turkey. It's huge. I just took it out to thaw, and I can marinate it tomorrow."

"Great, let me ask them and get back to you later. That should be fine…"

Maria liked the idea of not having to fix dinner, but she wasn't sure if mixing two families was the best idea…or how the boys or even David might interpret it.

At seven o'clock, she called her father knowing that he was an early riser. She told him about the rescue operation and explained she hadn't called earlier because there wasn't any cell service.

"Papi, I thought so much about you and the stories you told me during the *balseros* crisis."

"Yeah, but it seems like your supposed 'castaway' was a son of a…"

"I know. That's why I'm so mad about all the wasted time and effort…"

"That's part of the job, *mija*…"

She asked her father if they should accept David's invitation for Thanksgiving.

"I'd love to! But offer to make the stuffing for him. Nobody's tastes better than yours."

"That's not it, Papi, it's just that I don't know…"

Her father always knew how to read her thoughts.

"*Mariita*, where's the harm in two families with boys the same age celebrating dinner together? You're not signing a contract for life. Don't fret the small things. David is a good friend and colleague. Whatever happens next is up to God…"

Her father couldn't see that Maria's eyes had teared up. She was thankful that in the last few years she could keep having conversations with him that she previously would've only had with her mother.

When she got to the office at eight o'clock, Keppler was already at his desk. She poked her head in to greet him, and he invited her in to have a seat.

"Thanks, *Mariita*. Everyone did good work on this case and even though it looks like we've lost some time and resources, there was no other way to do it. I know the pending case is what's on your mind. Here, this arrived by email from Cuba. I printed it for you to read."

Keppler handed her some papers.

"Take these to your desk. Sometimes you might have to read between the lines. Let's see if you read it the same way I did."

Duquesne carefully read the ten-plus page file. She came to three important conclusions: in effect, Lazo's real name was Alberto Gonzalez, and he was seventeen when he left Cuba. A year before, he had been expelled from school for "ideological diversionism" and was sent to the fields to work. There were charges pending against him for selling horsemeat. Maria wasn't sure what the cause of his "ideological diversionism" was. The papers mentioned that he listened to the Beatles, had long hair, wore baggy pants, and that he had put a little paper boat out to sail on a puddle of water! All of this seemed more fictitious than any work by Padura, and she thought that if she could avoid it, she'd prefer not to travel to Cuba in the current climate. She thought she had all the information she needed. The couple was blackmailing Lazo (or Gonzalez) because they had provided him with falsified papers when he was young, and he didn't want his criminal record known, even though the charges against him were absurd. Still, this didn't prove that they had killed him.

As soon as Fernandez arrived half an hour later, they sat down together to compare notes. From the calls her colleague made they knew that Soledad and her daughter, Sole, had lived in various cities. They never stayed in one for more than two or three years and never left a trace of where they would be going next or a forwarding address. He had finally figured out that *El Oso*'s real name was Manuel Garcia—or maybe that was yet another alias—and that there had not been any activity on his social security number since 1994. Odalys—the woman who had taken care of Sole—had told Maria that they were living somewhere in the New York area, so Fernandez looked for death certificates and accident and missing persons reports until he finally found the information. Manuel Garcia had died in a strange accident. He had fallen off the ferry from Staten Island to Manhattan. The notice in the newspaper showed the widow with her face covered by a handkerchief and a child with her face hidden in her mother's jacket. Nevertheless, they identified them as

Soledad Garcia and her daughter Soledad Alexandra. This information coincided with the rumors that *El Oso* had died and explained why Soledad would have left New York so quickly. Maybe she had changed her last name?

Suddenly, an idea emerged from some dark corner of her mind and she called her father:

"Hey Papi, who was the guy known as the 'King of the Cuban countryside'?"

"*Mija,* always asking such strange questions…he was a man who kidnapped the rich to take their money and buy weapons during the wars for Independence. Some people thought of him as a hero, others as a bandit."

"A type of creole Robin Hood…"

"More or less," her father chuckled.

"What was his name?"

"Manuel Garcia. Why do you ask?"

Now Maria was certain that *El Oso* had also used an alias.

Chapter 20

Day 23—Tuesday, November 24, 2015

Maria felt content and well rested. Last night she had spoken with Patrick and then accepted David's invitation.

"You realize you're going to be the only woman among five guys?"

"As long as you don't expect me to wash all the dishes…"

"No, none of that, we're going to spoil you and wait on you, just like you do for everyone else all year long."

Maria smiled. There was so much enthusiasm in David's voice! She hung up and went to Publix to buy all the ingredients for the stuffing.

Next, she headed to the station with that same uneasiness in her stomach that she always felt when making progress on a case. She had a feeling that they were going to find the lost girl very soon.

What must he want now? she asked herself when her phone rang, and she saw that it was Bill.

"If you don't have plans, I would really like it if Patrick spent Thanksgiving with me this year…"

"Sorry Bill, but it's my turn this year and we have plans."

"If you're going to be at home, could I swing by for a bit?"

"No, we won't be there…"

"And what about your father's place?"

"He won't be home either, and besides, I'm done explaining things to you."

"Don't be that way. I have the right to know where my son will be spending such an important day... He isn't old enough to..."

"What? First of all, you don't have the right. Second, you can't think that I would take him anywhere dangerous or indecent. And third, you've gone your whole life saying he's old enough to be more independent, and now..."

"Ok, ok I get it... You woke up on the wrong side of the bed today."

"Not at all. I was perfectly fine until you called. And look, if you want to see him Thanksgiving Day and you can manage to get him up early enough, you two can have breakfast together, but he needs to be back before three o'clock."

The dinner at David's house wasn't until five o'clock, but Maria knew how Bill tended to run late when it came to these things.

"No, I was hoping he could come with me and have dinner somewhere."

"So he could meet somebody special?" Maria asked maliciously.

"Well, kind of..."

"It'll have to wait. Maybe he can go Friday... He goes back to school early Saturday for the football game in Gainesville."

"Come on Maria, this is important to me. I'll trade you Thanksgiving for Christmas."

"I would do it if I could Bill, but I also want him to meet someone special, and we've already made plans."

This wasn't entirely true because Patrick already knew David well, but she wanted to irritate her ex-husband.

"Fine, have a good time!" he yelled and hung up the phone without saying goodbye.

When Maria got to the station, her good mood had changed. And, to make things worse, Fernandez had been assigned to another case and wouldn't be at the office for the entire day. She had thought about trying to put together a timeline of all their leads and a chronology of everything they already knew, but she preferred to do it with him. What's more, Fernandez's handwriting was chicken scratch, and although he had left his notes, it was difficult to read them.

She decided to call Gladys Elena Lazo and to go see her in Hialeah. On the phone, she told her they didn't have any concrete news, just a few leads, so that she wouldn't get her hopes up.

At that hour of the morning the woman was alone and welcomed Maria with a traditional Cuban coffee. When they finally sat down, Maria told her point-blank:

"Look Gladys, I'm not going to turn on the recorder. Last time we saw each other, I got the impression that you were hiding something from me. It might seem insignificant to you, but you never know what might be useful in solving the case."

The woman seemed troubled, but answered firmly.

"I'm not sure why you have that impression. I have no reason to lie to you… What do you think about my mother's dream?"

"Well, for the police a dream isn't evidence…but we have other leads. I'd like to ask you something."

"Yes?"

"We finally received the DNA results for your husband Lazo."

Maria didn't want to reveal that his real last name was Gonzalez.

"It took quite a while didn't it?"

"Yes, but these types of tests can take a long time and that's why I wanted to ask for your authorization for someone to come tomorrow at a time that works for you to take a DNA sample from your saliva."

"What for?" asked the woman with a touch of uneasiness in her voice.

"Well, I don't want to give you any false hopes, but if we find someone who we think could be your daughter, before you can know for sure, we have to run DNA tests to confirm that you and Lazo are her parents. The wait will be shorter if we already have your DNA. Perhaps you could also give me something of the baby's to extract DNA. Maybe if you have a little hairbrush?"

"But have you found someone?"

"Not yet."

"Then?"

"This is so we can be prepared."

"It's not a problem, they can come tomorrow."

The woman had a worried look on her face and Maria didn't want to leave until she found out what secret she was hiding.

Indeed, after an awkward silence, the woman covered her face with her hands and began sobbing.

Maria let her cry for a moment before saying:

"I can't even imagine the stress and pain over all these years… I didn't want to give you any false hope…"

Finally, Gladys stood up, left the room, and returned blowing her nose with a Kleenex and confidentially, told Maria:

"You're a wonderful detective. It's true, I haven't told you the whole truth. No one knows what I'm about to tell you, not a single soul."

"Tell me, I won't record it or take notes. I'm only going to keep in mind what can help me with the case."

"The baby isn't Ray's…"

Maria wasn't surprised. What's more, she suspected it from the beginning.

"Is it your husband's?"

"Yes, how did you know?"

"Instincts that we develop as detectives… Tell me what happened and why you've lied for all these years."

"Well, I was a virgin, but on the night before I left Cuba, Mauricio and I made love for the first time. When I realized I was pregnant, I didn't know what to do. My mother hadn't come from Cuba yet, and Raulito and I were alone in this country. I learned that Mauricio was going out with someone else and, in any case, how was he going to help me all the way from Pinar del Rio? That's when I met Ray. I wasn't sure if I should tell you, but he was so in love with me and so anxious to protect me that I didn't think twice about getting married to him. That's why people thought the baby was born early. I couldn't have told my mother because she still believed in the old-fashioned ways, that women should be virgins when they get married. Besides, she would've told Mauricio. Ray was so happy with the little girl…and later, after they disappeared and Mauricio finally came here and we got married, how was I going to tell him? He would've thought I didn't know how to take care of our daughter… He would've held it against me for not telling him… In the long run, I thought it was better to continue with the lie. I don't know if that was the right thing to do. Maybe if he had known she was his, he would've helped me with the search all these years."

"And no one knows this?"

"You can't imagine, apart from the uncertainty of not knowing whether my daughter is alive or not, the weight of carrying a secret like this for so many years…"

"I know, it's a heavy burden…but eventually you'll have to tell him."

"If we find her, yes, but I think then he'll be happy and forgive me."

"You don't think he suspects anything?"

"Him? No, you know how clueless men are when it comes to these things. And surprisingly enough, my mother doesn't either, and she's so clever. She thinks I had sex with Ray before getting married. But you know who I think does suspect something? My daughter Elena... I don't know, I just have a hunch."

"It's because they look so much alike, and they're both identical to your husband."

"That's true, perhaps that's the reason why, but I don't think she's ever been certain and maybe that's for the best. It's difficult to explain to your kids that you've lied over so many years."

Maria stood up when she saw that Gladys, although worried, seemed relieved after revealing her secret. She also asked her if she could have her husband's hairbrush or toothbrush so she could extract some DNA and told her that they would come for her saliva sample tomorrow. It was the fastest and safest way.

"I'll give you his toothbrush... I have two new ones and can replace both his and mine. I do that occasionally so he won't suspect anything... I'll look for my daughter's as well. I have all her things safely stored in a box."

"The most important part is that we find your daughter, Gladys. Everything else will work itself out."

This time, Gladys Elena Lazo said goodbye to Detective Duquesne with a strong hug.

Chapter 21

Day 24—Wednesday, November 25, 2015

The first thing that Maria did when she got to the station was call Odalys Fuentes, the woman who had taken care of Sole in New York. She wanted to know if she remembered where Soledad had worked so that maybe she could get her social security number, or at least the one she used back then. She suspected that the woman had learned the art of falsifying documents from her partner. It wasn't going to be easy to trace Soledad's steps; at any rate, she got through to Odalys's answering machine. She left various messages, but the woman never responded to any of them. She presumed that maybe, like so many people, she was at some relative's house for Thanksgiving, the busiest travel day in the United States.

Her own office was half-empty and quiet since many were preparing the big family dinner for the next day. Traffic was another story. Shopping centers, in particular ones with stores like Publix, Winn Dixie, or Costco, were especially jam-packed. The lines at the Honey Baked Ham stores were impressive too. The take-out places were equally full. Many Cubans typically substituted a pork shoulder for turkey. Others marinated the bird with *mojo criollo* and served it with black beans and rice instead of the traditional mashed or sweet potatoes.

Fernandez would not be coming back until Monday, and Maria decided that she shouldn't wait too long to organize all the leads they had. She had begun reading her notes when her cell rang. It was from Kendall Hospital. Joaquin del Roble had asked to see her. Fearing that he had gotten worse, Maria didn't waste any time getting in her car and going to see him.

Contrary to her fears, she found him sitting up and looking much better than he did when she saw him a few days ago. They greeted each other like old friends. Maria asked him about his health:

"Well, it looks like I won't die from this... I'm better, or at least that's what they say..."

"You look good."

"I think I saw you on TV in the rescue efforts for that guy who faked his own death."

"Yes, it was a waste of time and resources, and it has put me a little behind on the case, just when we're starting to get solid leads."

Maria told him what she had found out about Alberto Gonzalez from the Cuban police; however, she didn't tell him the new information they had about the girl since she now knew they weren't blood relatives.

"Look, Detective Duquesne, I couldn't finish my story for you before, and it probably would have saved you some work."

"I'm all ears."

Maria took out her notepad and recorder, and del Roble consented with a nod.

"I was already aware of what you've figured out...more or less... The thing is when they found Alberto's body in the canal, I looked up his mother's phone number in Cuba. I felt that I had a duty to let her know. She was inconsolable and kept repeating, 'But what he did here was just child's play. He didn't deserve to get kicked out of school...he was just a kid.' That part puzzled me. That same night I called her again with the pretense of seeing if she had calmed down. This time I asked her for her son's full name and date of birth. I told her it was for the obituary and the death certificate. That's when I realized that his name was neither Raimundo nor Lazo and also that he was actually seventeen when he arrived. At the moment, I didn't make the connection that they had falsified papers for him or that they had blackmailed him, and that as a result he was forced to give them information about me that led to my attack. I didn't figure that out until much later. Regardless, that didn't change my opinion of him as a good kid. When I spoke with Alberto's mother, and she told me even more things that her mother had told her about my brother, I was certain that he was my great-nephew. Alberto's wife had just arrived from Cuba, and they were broke…"

"So that's why you paid for the funeral?"

"Yes, that's why, and I don't know, because of a certain family honor, out of an obligation to my brother. How would I have felt if they had thrown him in a common grave?"

"You're a very good man, Don Joaquin."

"Come on, don't exaggerate. A few dollars more or less don't matter at my age. The important thing is to have a clear conscience. Don't you think?"

"Yes…and that's why I'd like to do something for you."

Del Roble looked deep in thought.

"Detective Duquesne, you don't owe me anything."

There was a brief silence, and then Maria saw that sparkle in his eyes and that old Spaniard's devilish grin that she had seen before.

"I know what you want! Are you sure it won't harm you?"

"Of course not, and even less if you join me."

Maria looked at the time.

"Don't you think it's a little early?"

"Truth be told, yes. It would be better after the nap."

"Well then, I'll return at that hour, but I won't be able to stay long."

"I know. You probably have to cook for your family. But I am going to appreciate it very much."

Before going back to the station, she stopped by her father's house for a moment since it was on her way. She took some turkey slices and a Greek yogurt out of the refrigerator and ate it while listening to the news on CNN and her father's comments about football teams. In spite of her son's love for this sport and now her father's, Maria still didn't understand it, but hearing her father's enthusiastic tone pleased her.

When she got back to the office, Keppler asked her to lend him a hand in a fraud case they were investigating. They had arrested a woman in Puerto Rico for using a false birth certificate to apply for a US passport and a driver's license in Florida. They were trying to determine whether it was an isolated case or part of a larger scam.

Maria worked for a few hours gathering information on passport applications, but at four in the afternoon Keppler himself suggested that she take off and wished her a happy Thanksgiving.

A half an hour later she was back with Joaquin del Roble. In her purse, she had a small bottle of whiskey. They drank it from paper cups, and the Spaniard became nostalgic remembering his native land. He even sang old songs that his grandmother had taught him as a child.

Maria wanted to be back at the house when Patrick and his friend arrived, so, despite having a good time and feeling bad leaving the old man alone, she said goodbye and promised that she would visit him again soon. She was sincere. She had grown fond of the old Spaniard.

She hadn't been home half an hour when she heard Patrick open the door, and she ran to hug him.

Immediately she asked:

"And your friend, didn't he come?"

"Yes, Mami. But heads up, it's not a guy. It's a girl."

"Oh!"

"*I told you, a friend,*" he emphasized in English.

"Yes, you're right. I was the one who assumed it was a guy."

"Mami, she's really just a friend. We don't have any other type of relationship, but she didn't have anywhere to go. I'll explain later."

As the adorable girl came in, Maria assumed she was African American at first, but later learned she was Haitian.

Patrick told her to take his room and that he would sleep on the couch in the study.

The kids had already eaten on the road, so the girl, who seemed shy, went right to her room.

Maria and Patrick stayed in the kitchen. She had a cup of tea while he downed a huge glass of milk.

The mother knew her son well. She didn't ask him any questions. She sipped her hot tea and finally looked him in the eyes tenderly where she saw a budding sparkle of passion. Patrick began to speak, slowly at first:

"Mami, I met Mathilda at the beginning of the semester. We have a history class together. You can't imagine how smart and sensitive she is and what she has gone through in her life. I admit that I didn't know anything about Haiti, even though so many Haitians live here in Miami and we always hear when they drown in boats in the ocean… I'm not saying I understand all of this now, although the course we're taking is about Caribbean history. Despite being shy, Mathilda argues with the professor because obviously she knows more about her country than he does, just like I know more about Cuba… During the political violence that they experienced there, when Mathilda was about eight, in 2004 I think, they killed her grandfather."

Now Patrick began to speak more quickly, gushing, as if he needed to get out something very painful:

"The worst part was the 2010 earthquake. She was buried under rubble for almost a week. It was a miracle that they found her alive! And the entire time, she was there with her grandmother beside her, who was injured and then later she died, with her head resting on Mathilda's shoulder. Can you imagine? When they rescued her she set out to search for her parents, but she never found them. She still doesn't know if they're dead or alive, although she has come to accept the worst. For three years she was living from house to house with different relatives until an uncle who was able to come to the United States took her to New York, where he lives with his family. Imagine getting used to that fast-paced city after only living in Haiti! She tells me that she has forgotten a lot of things but more than anything the ability to express her emotions. In addition to the love of her aunts, uncles, and cousins, she says that what saved her was her studies because she always wanted to get a good education. When she graduated from high school, they offered her various scholarships, and she chose the one from the University of Florida because she doesn't like the cold at all… Little by little she's been getting stronger, but she still has a weekly session with the psychiatrist via Skype…"

"The things you can do in the modern world!" exclaimed Maria.

The comment relieved the tension a little. Maria listened to Mathilda's story and thought about how the same thing had happened to Joaquin del Roble and Rosa Blass, how so many people had suffered so much, and how Cubans believed that they were the only ones who had lived through a national tragedy. Besides, the story about the young girl who was now sleeping in her son's bed moved her, and she felt proud that Patrick felt empathy and solidarity for Mathilda.

"I invited her to come because her uncle couldn't pay for the ticket for her to go to New York for four days… I knew that you would understand."

She didn't know what to say. She stood up. Patrick did the same.

"Mami, we have so many things to thankful for…"

They embraced each other in silence.

Chapter 22

Day 25—Thursday, November 26, 2015

Patrick and Mathilda entered the kitchen at the same time. Both gave Maria a kiss. It was uncommon for Americans to greet one another so affectionately, but the culture of Haiti where the girl had grown up was another thing. Maria offered to fix them breakfast, but Patrick explained that he had unfortunately agreed to have it with his dad. She saw them leave holding hands. The contrast of her son's very white skin and the girl's dark skin was…Maria didn't know how to describe it…a little shocking. She knew that it wouldn't matter in the least to her father, but perhaps she should give David a heads up. Then she thought about the shock that it would be for her ex-husband Bill, and she started laughing so hard that the sadness felt by Mathilda's story turned into great joy because she would be able to spend that day with so many loved ones.

She searched for a classical music channel on the television and got ready to lay out on the countertop all the ingredients for her famous turkey stuffing: the Italian sausages, the package of Pepperidge Farm corn stuffing, Swanson's chicken broth, apples, butter, onions, celery, nuts, cranberries and the spices: salt, pepper, thyme, parsley, and sage. Even though the recipe didn't call for it, she added dry wine. It seemed like she could hear her mother's voice:

"Rare is the dish that doesn't improve with a little dry wine."

This time, while she went about things, Maria photographed the mixture of ingredients. She had a Facebook page with a fake name that only a few friends knew. Police officers were not permitted to post their private life publicly, but she thought documenting the process of cooking her son's favorite dish was one way for him to make it in the future. She was glad that these days the roles of men and women weren't as defined as before. She could picture Patrick cooking with as much ease as if he were a girl.

When she finished, it smelled great, but half the kitchen and a pile of pots and pans were dirty. She scrubbed, cleaned, went through her email, read the newspaper, and watched some of the Macy's parade on television until it was time to shower and get dressed. She wanted to be ready ahead of time because she knew that her father would arrive early and that at the last minute Patrick would ask her to iron him a shirt or sew on a button that he had lost. As it turned out, the old man did arrive beforehand but her son didn't need anything from her. He and Mathilda were ready right on time. Maria didn't want to arrive too early, and she thought it would be a good idea to try to ease Mathilda into things a bit before she had to meet the others at David's. She asked her whether she spoke French and Mathilda nodded. Maria made an effort to remember a language she studied for many years but hardly ever practiced. Patrick looked at her amazed while Maria spoke French animatedly with the girl whose face seemed to light up.

They took a few pictures before heading to David's house. Her father brought two bottles of wine, and Patrick carried the big casserole dish with the stuffing.

"You're going to eat something delicious…nobody makes it like my mom," he told Mathilda.

When they were in the car, Lourdes called her. She was giddy.

"Oh, *Mariita*, you were right. I know that you've probably already seen it on television, that's why I didn't call earlier. Anyway, we had a good time and stayed a few days in New York, but if you're going to be home, I'll stop by and drop off a few things."

Maria explained that they were on their way to celebrate Thanksgiving with friends, and they agreed to get together soon.

David and his kids received them as if it were the most natural thing in the world, even though she had forgotten to tell her colleague about Mathilda. It surprised her how nicely the table was set and how organized everything was. After a few drinks and snacks, the adults chatted and the others watched football in the den until David and his kids began working in the kitchen. They didn't let her come in, not even when she said she needed to heat up the stuffing.

"We've got this."

Fifteen minutes later, everything was set up on a table adjacent to the one in the dining room: the platter with sliced turkey and other dishes with sweet potatoes, stuffing, and another with green beans and crispy onions. There was also an appetizing salad and a basket with warm dinner rolls.

David was telling everyone their place at the table and asked:

"Who wants to say grace?"

It surprised her that her son volunteered.

Everyone joined hands.

After Patrick finished giving thanks for the food, good health, loved ones, freedom, and the good fortune they all enjoyed, his voice cracked when he prayed for those less fortunate.

Maria realized the impact that his friendship with Mathilda had had on him. Secretly, she thanked God for having a son like Patrick.

The food was delicious, the kids happy. Maria was glad she had accepted David's invitation. Actually, there were many things for which she was thankful that Thursday in November. Nevertheless, although she was trying to put it out of her mind, the same thought kept haunting her: it was one more holiday that Gladys Elena Lazo celebrated without her daughter.

Chapter 23

Day 29—Monday, November 30, 2015

The long weekend had been a much-needed break. Maria couldn't remember feeling that happy in a long time. She had enjoyed dinner at David's house, the time she spent with Patrick and Mathilda during the short period they were home, the lunch and the movies that she had watched on TV with her father on Saturday, and David's long visit on Sunday after his kids returned to their mother's house.

Nevertheless, she was anxious to get back to work and the unresolved case. She promised herself that if Gladys Mercedes was alive, as she believed, she would find her before the end of the year. Secretly, she had resolved that the mother and daughter would spend Christmas together. At times, however, a lot of questions hounded her. What if the girl had been corrupted by the kidnappers and was taking part in criminal acts? Or, on the contrary, what if they had treated Soledad well, and she didn't know that she had been abducted, and she rejected her real family? *That isn't your task right now*, she said to herself. *Your job is to find her*. But she couldn't get those types of ideas out of her head.

She arrived at the police station early and, not long after, Fernandez came in with a cup of coffee. They didn't waste much time making small talk about what they had done during the holiday. Both were eager to get back on organizing the clues. Maria began by getting him up to speed on what she had found out about Alberto Gonzalez:

"Look, Fernandez, for the moment I don't think we should waste any more time looking into him. We'll only look into things if the falsified documents or robberies in his uncle's house and business lead us to Manuel Garcia and Soledad."

"Yeah, you're right. In any case, it's going to be really difficult to find out when and how these two entered the US since they could've been able to use countless aliases."

"That's why we should concentrate on the events that happened after Garcia's death. Don't you think? I'll call the woman back who babysat for Sole during that time."

"And I'll call her old teacher in Tampa. I'll also follow up with the two or three people that had left us a message after we sent out the sketches."

"I have some people that I need to check with too."

Maria finally got in touch with Odalys in New Jersey. She had received the sketches and confirmed that they indeed were of Soledad and her daughter.

"Look, I can't be sure about the man because I hardly ever saw him. I think he only came by once to pick up the girl because Soledad was late getting home from work."

"And do you know where she worked?"

"Let me see if I remember…it's been a long time…it had something to do with sewing… I don't know if it was in a factory or in a store where they did alterations. She sewed very well. She made some lovely dresses for the girl."

Maria was persistent with her questions. She wanted to know if she remembered which district she worked in, if she knew which neighborhood they lived in, if she had saved their old phone number, if she had any bit of information at all that might help her.

"I honestly would like to help you because I'd love to know what happened to them, but after her husband died in the accident, it was as if they vanished. Look, the only thing that comes to mind is that a neighbor's daughter plays that sport where you pass a black and white ball with your feet. What do you call it?"

"Soccer?"

"Yeah, that's it...*fútbol* is called soccer here because 'football' is something else... Once she went with her school to play I don't know where, I think in North or South Carolina, and she came across Sole. It was like four or five years after they left here."

"And Sole also played soccer?"

"Yeah... I think so."

"And this neighbor of yours, does she still live nearby?"

"No, they moved a long time ago, and I've also lost track of them too..."

"Well, if you remember something else, anything at all, if you find a phone number, a picture, anything, call me. Can you promise me that?"

"Of course, you can count on it."

Duquesne dialed one of the phone numbers in Manhattan that she hadn't reached the last time. Mrs. Jonathan didn't speak Spanish, but she had recognized the sketches that had been circulating in the press. She was now retired, but she had taken part in the investigation of the accident in which Manuel Garcia had died.

She told Maria that the details of the accident weren't entirely clear. The ferry had hit the pier just before docking, and the man was leaning on the railing, so he fell into the water on impact, hit his head, and died instantly. At first, it seemed that the captain was to blame because they found some beer cans, but the blood test showed that he wasn't intoxicated.

They wanted to interview the widow, but she had left without a trace. Little by little, the case became cold. In an attempt to find her, they checked with the Social Security office to see if she had filed a claim, which would have been within her right since she had a young child, but there was nothing pending in the system.

"Also, I called a friend of mine and asked her to look in the archives, and I was able to get Manuel Garcia's social security number for you. I thought that might help you."

Maria thanked her profusely, although she was more interested in finding Soledad and her daughter than investigating the dead husband's past.

She decided to make one last call before contacting the Social Security office.

She talked to Altagracia Pena, a Dominican woman who was over eighty years old. According to what she told Maria, she had been Soledad's friend from work. She confirmed the same story of how she had left without saying goodbye or collecting her last check when her husband died. They sewed together in a factory. There were undocumented immigrants who they paid in cash, but Soledad had her green card and was on the payroll. They had even made her a supervisor.

Maria asked her the name of the factory. The woman tried to remember.

"Hmm, it's been a long time…the business was named after the owner, a Latino last name. Rodriguez Shoes and Apparel…or Perez, or Lopez…a common last name…perhaps Martinez…"

The Dominican woman pointed out the metro stop where she got off and the streets that she had to walk.

"But the factory closed a while ago…there's nothing left of it. There was a big fire about fifteen years ago. I had just retired. Anyway it was at night and no one was inside…"

It seemed to Maria like all of the clues were dead ends. She was about to see where Manuel Garcia's social security number would lead her when she saw Fernandez running toward her, waving his arms and repeating:

"I think I found Sole!"

Sure enough, a second conversation with her teacher in Tampa and other calls to the high school where Sole had been a student had yielded some results. The contacts at the high school had emailed the diploma of Soledad A. Garcia, who had graduated on June 4, 2010, along with her address and phone number from the school directory.

"Let me guess. They've moved away, and no one knows where they are?"

Fernandez nodded.

"But it's a good clue, Maria, because they're also looking for the colleges that she applied to... We're going to find her, you'll see." He encouraged her and took a sip of the cold coffee that was left in the white Styrofoam cup.

Chapter 24

Days 30 and 31—Tuesday and Wednesday, December 1 and 2, 2015

Maria and Fernandez worked nonstop, obsessing over each clue. As they had imagined, Manuel Garcia's social security number belonged to a person who had already passed away, and it didn't lead them to much. However, with the help of some friends, they had managed to get the FBI to use their digital facial recognition system, and they found out that Manuel Garcia's real name was Bruno Marron (alias *El Oso*), and that he had a criminal record for fraud, bad checks, and robbery, but no violent crimes. Also, the FBI records included an investigation into his links with the Cuban government, but it had been closed when he died. Maria thought that maybe that explained how he knew what the Mariel refugees wanted to hide and, more importantly, his ability to falsify Cuban documents.

Aldo del Pozo had provided Maria with a list of four people who remembered the couple in Fort Chaffee. Two of them confessed that he had arranged for them to get copies of their college transcripts.

"Look, I don't know if they were falsified, but the signatures and grades matched the real ones. I didn't think twice about using them because they were proof of my degree and allowed me to continue my career. They cost me a lot. Luckily my father had been here for a while, and he paid him," a woman who had been able to finish medical school told Maria.

Another told Fernandez a similar story and said that he had paid five hundred dollars for the transcript. *El Oso* hadn't tried to extort them in either case. The detectives concluded that maybe these documents were legitimate and that the man had been able to get them from the Cuban government.

Fernandez looked for colleges that had women's soccer teams thinking that perhaps Sole had received a scholarship to play for one of them. He was surprised to see that there were more than three hundred teams. He patiently searched through the websites of each team, each of the player's names, and the team pictures, inspecting every one of their faces in case the girl had changed her name. If she had graduated high school in 2010, obviously it would make sense that she would have already finished her four years of college. The first thing that the young detective discovered was that college websites don't emphasize their women's sports teams. He indignantly told this to Maria. There were photos of various teams online, and some from prior years when Sole may have played, but they didn't have names. He had to look through them face by face in order to see if anyone looked like her. It was like looking for a needle in a haystack. Additionally, they weren't even sure if she played soccer, much less that she had played in college. It was only a hunch based on the information from her friend in New Jersey who had seen her in the Carolinas.

By eight in the evening, the two detectives were exhausted and decided they would start up again in the morning.

Fernandez tried to lift Maria's spirits:

"Sometimes, when you stop thinking, a new idea appears out of nowhere. That happens to me every time."

She nodded and went to the gym even though she was worn out. Sometimes working out helped her sleep better and wake up with a new perspective, as if ideas appeared from her subconscious while she slept.

Sure enough, after talking briefly with David and her father and taking a shower, she went to bed without even eating dinner.

The next morning while she drank her coffee, watched CNN, and read *The Miami Herald*, she received a text from Fernandez.

"Good clues from Sole's high school."

She got to the police station as fast as she could. Fernandez was already at the computer, rechecking photo after photo. He explained that the school had given them the names of the colleges to which Sole had applied, although they didn't know which one she had attended.

Maria kept on making calls and looking for clues, but was unsuccessful. It was almost noon when Fernandez waved her over to his computer.

He showed her a photo of the 2011 soccer team at Notre Dame. He enlarged it and zoomed in on one of the young women.

"What do you think?"

"It's her, Fernandez, it's her."

Maria noticed that the building was made of gray bricks, just like the one in Sole's grandmother's dream. She didn't believe in those types of things and chose not to tell her partner.

"Let's call the university immediately. She should have already graduated, but I'm sure they'll have her address."

They called the alumni office and sent emails, but the staff only agreed to look for her information and talk with their lawyers to see if they could share it.

Fernandez continued his search online until he found the 2012 Notre Dame roster. At first, he was worried when he didn't see her name. The woman who he believed to be Soledad Garcia wore number fifty-six, which corresponded to an Alexis Smith. Had he been wrong?

He asked Maria to come over once again. They enlarged the photo. They looked at all of the sketches they had of the girl. They also compared them with the photos they had of her sister Elena. Each time they became more certain that they were dealing with the same person.

"Let's do the easy thing. Let's look for Alexis Smith on Facebook."

They found her but, without sending a friend request, they only had access to minimal information. She had graduated from Notre Dame, was living in Tampa, was married, and had a young daughter.

"Do you think it's the same woman?" Maria asked aloud.

"Well, if she got married it's logical that she would change her last name. The high school diploma said Soledad A. Garcia, and we know from the newspaper article that Sole's middle name was Alexandra, so maybe she decided to go by Alexis," reasoned Fernandez. "It makes sense that she would be in Tampa if she lived there before…"

"But not if her mother's alive. They've been bouncing around from place to place for years," speculated Maria.

"And what if her mother's dead? That hadn't dawned on us because she wouldn't be that old, but as they say 'in order to die you only have to be alive.' " As soon as he said that, Fernandez started looking for obituaries for women named Soledad Garcia. He was surprised to find five in the last six years. Two were in Miami and were about women over eighty years old, so he discarded them. The third was about a young woman who had died in a car accident two days before her eighteenth birthday and high school graduation in Arizona. The fourth and fifth made him think: a sixty-year-old woman in Tampa who had died in 2010 and, the other, a fifty-one-year-old who had passed away the following year in South Bend, Indiana. Both could be the one they were looking for, but the obituaries gave limited information.

Meanwhile, Maria had been tracing Alexis's steps at Notre Dame and in Tampa. An hour later, she went to look for Fernandez at his desk, her eyes full of that special sparkle that they got when she felt close to solving a case.

"Come take a look…"

She showed him a photo that she had found in the Notre Dame newspaper from the day of Alexis Smith's graduation. A young girl whose face could only be partially seen was hugging her. Dressed in her cap and gown, the graduate was carrying the little girl and smiling at the camera. The article described how, despite having taken care of her mother during her cancer and later her death and having given birth to her own daughter, all within the first two years of college, Alexis had graduated with honors.

Maria had also tracked down the records of residential properties in Tampa and discovered that Nicholas and Alexis Smith had bought a house only a few months previously. Neither had a criminal record, and Maria showed Fernandez a photo of the house where they were living.

"It's incredible what you can find online these days. You should've seen how it used to be…" Maria commented to her colleague.

"Don't pretend to be an old lady…and don't change the subject. Are we sure that it's her? What do we do now?"

"I'd like to go see her, but we have to talk to Larry first."

They both ran directly to their boss's office.

Chapter 25

Days 32 and 33—Thursday and Friday, December 3 and 4, 2015

The previous day, Lawrence Keppler had been out of the office all day in meetings on criminal activities in the county. By mid-afternoon, he had contacted his assistant and asked her to call together all officers for a meeting at nine in the morning.

Maria and Fernandez knew that they'd have to wait before they could speak with him and request authorization to travel to Tampa.

Keppler came into the conference room with a bulky black folder under his arm and accompanied by Captain Rios. The meeting had something to do with a workshop on new equipment and the most advanced technology that they were about to start using soon. They were on a coffee break when Keppler's and Rios's cells rang in unison. Both answered at the same time, and then they left the room to be able to hear better. They returned right away.

"I've just been informed that one man is dead and two others injured," Keppler said when he came back into the room.

Seconds later Rios entered:

"The man they shot this morning over a parking place just died."

Keppler and Rios cancelled the meeting. The captain left quickly and Keppler started assigning tasks to various officers.

Without realizing it, Maria and Fernandez had become a team and they were sent to the crime scene. They knew they had to follow orders and that the case of the girl that they believed they'd found would have to wait. When they arrived at the house in the northwest part of the county, it was surrounded by yellow tape, as was typically the case. The photographer and the coroner were already inside, next to the body of a young man lying on the floor with a hole in his chest and a large bloodstain. Outside, paramedics treated two young women for minor injuries while they waited for an ambulance to take them to the hospital. One of them was crying inconsolably. She was the victim's wife. An older man, who turned out to be the girls' father and who had also been inside the house during the episode, was trying to comfort her.

Maria made a gesture to Fernandez for him to question the other girl, and she tried to calm down the widow and her father so that they could tell her what had happened. The woman took a deep breath, dried her tears with the back of her hand, and began speaking.

"It was my fault… How could I have opened the door for them? Who would think that they would do such a thing at ten in the morning?" she exclaimed and began crying again. Maria waited a few seconds.

"What happened next?"

"The one that I saw was pretty young. He even looked familiar from the neighborhood, and he told me he was selling some chocolate to raise money for his baseball team. I love chocolate, and when I returned with the two dollars, I opened the door. The boy wasn't there anymore. Three other guys in hoodies came in, and they pushed me down. Then, my sister Alicia started screaming, and they threw her against the entranceway table, which is glass, and it broke. My husband heard the noise and came running in, the poor thing, armed with a broom. I imagine he thought we needed to clean up the glass…but it happened all so fast, and they shot him. They told us to give them all the jewelry and money that we had. I was terrified and couldn't move, and my sister was bleeding from the glass wounds. Then, my father came in and struggled with one of them. Alicia and I began screaming. I think the neighbor heard us and called the police. It looks like they got scared and left without taking anything. It would've been better if they had just taken everything and not killed my husband. We were newlyweds and so happy," the woman mumbled and began sobbing again.

A few moments later, the ambulances arrived and took the two sisters away. Their father wanted to go with them, and Maria agreed to let him go but first told him that she would stop by the hospital later to ask him more questions and so they could give her a description of the assailants. The forensic team looked for fingerprints, especially on the doorknob on the front door. They didn't find any. Apparently, the assailants had worn gloves. They didn't find the shell either, but the bullet might possibly show up when they performed the autopsy on the victim. It hadn't been a well-organized crime, but for now there were few clues.

At Maria's request, Fernandez called the station and asked for information on robberies and incidents in the area, regardless of how small they were. Next, both continued to interview the neighbors. The only one who said he'd seen anything was the man across the street. He described how the thieves were dressed in gray hoodies, drove a dark blue getaway truck, and even some numbers on the license plate.

The two detectives were eating hamburger for lunch at a nearby McDonald's when they received the information about criminal activities in the area. Mainly, the details were about a gang of young kids who had committed acts of vandalism, stolen radios and wheels off cars, but nothing violent. Headquarters sent them pictures of the gang members.

They went to the hospital to see the sisters and their father. Maria began by asking the widow to describe the boy who had tried to sell her chocolate. The woman thought hard.

"I saw him through the peephole. He had black hair across his forehead. He was very young. He even still had acne on his face!"

Next, Maria showed her the pictures on her phone one at a time. The woman looked at them carefully.

"No, that isn't him," she said four times. On the fifth, she exclaimed, "That's him…that's him, I'm certain."

Maria asked her if the boy was one of the ones in hoodies that entered the house.

"I don't think so because the three of them were taller, broader in the shoulders, a little older…this one is a young boy, and I can't place him, but I have the impression I've seen him before."

When Maria showed the pictures to Alicia, the other sister, who never saw the first boy, she immediately said:

"He works at Winn Dixie bagging groceries. He lives in the neighborhood."

A few hours later, they brought Lorenzo Febles into the station. He was under eighteen, so they couldn't question him without one of his parents present. They found his mother in the school cafeteria where she worked.

As soon as the woman arrived, the boy embraced her:

"Mami, I'm so sorry. I didn't know what they were going to do."

They didn't need to press too much for Lorenzo to confess. The three boys, who were older than him, belonged to a gang in a nearby neighborhood. He had not gone to school that morning because he didn't want to take a test that he hadn't studied for. He kept walking through the neighborhood until his mother left for work so that she wouldn't know. They came up to him with a box of chocolates and told him to help them. They said that he should ask for two dollars for each box, but they were going to give him ten dollars for each house that opened the door. This had been the first house where the woman had said yes, and, when she went to get the money, the other boys pushed him out of the way and went in as soon as she opened the door. He didn't like what was happening, and he took off running.

Fernandez doubted the story, but Maria believed it. First, the boy didn't have a single scrape on his arms or his clothing and, second, there was something in the mother's stern face, in the boy's distressed tone that convinced her. Either way, they would have to wait until they could confirm his version of the events. Lorenzo assured them that he didn't know the boys' names except he'd heard one of them called Manazas, and he knew where they typically hung out.

Before dark, they had arrested all three. Maria and Fernandez went back to the station to fill out the reports that would be key in order for the district attorney to press charges. Beforehand, they stopped by to see Dr. John Erwin, but the coroner hadn't yet begun the autopsy and would have to get back to them. Finally, they learned that they had extracted a 45-caliber bullet from the left lung. It had pierced his heart. They immediately ordered tests to see whether the bullet had been shot with the weapon found in a trash can halfway between the crime scene and the house where the three gang members lived.

It wasn't until Friday afternoon that they were able to turn in all the details to the district attorney so they could proceed with the case. Maria wondered whether she should discuss the trip to Tampa with Keppler or wait until after the weekend. She didn't have an option. When she went to his office the assistant told her that he'd left early and wasn't returning until Monday. *Maybe it'll do me good to rest a little over the weekend and reflect on how to get closer to the girl*, Maria thought, and she invited Fernandez out for a few beers.

"Two heads are better than one," she said. "Let's plan everything out for next week."

Fernandez accepted with enthusiasm.

Chapter 26

Days 34–36—Saturday through Monday, December 5 through 7, 2015

Maria hadn't left the house all weekend. She was glad that David had gone to spend the weekend away with his kids, and that her father believed the little white lie that she'd told him—that she was in bed with a migraine. She did suffer from those terrible headaches, and, even though she hadn't recently had one of those episodes that made her lie down and close all the windows to keep out the light, she still wasn't completely herself. She felt an increasing stress regarding the idea of going to speak with Alexis Smith. If she didn't turn out to be Gladys Mercedes, the visit would be brief, and they'd have to keep on looking. However, if it were the same person, would she know her own true identity? Would she agree to a DNA test? Had she led a happy life with her husband and young child, and was Maria about to turn it all upside down?

On Sunday afternoon, she showered, fixed herself up, took a bottle of whiskey from her bar, hid it in a gift bag with two disposable plastic glasses, and went to see Joaquin del Roble. She found him sitting in a chair with a blanket on his lap reading. He tried to stand up when he saw her come in.

"Please, don't get up."

She approached him and extended her hand, which he kissed in that gallant gesture that moved Maria so much.

"I should've called first," she apologized.

"On the contrary, this way I'm surprised, and the pleasure of seeing you is doubled."

"Tripled…because of what I've brought you," she said and showed him the bag that she'd hidden.

After they spent a few minutes enjoying their drinks in silence, Don Joaquin said to her:

"You're worried… Can I help with something?"

It was then that she realized that, in fact, she'd grown close to that simple yet wise little old man and come to rely on his advice. She smiled at him.

"You know me well. Yes, I am worried. Listen, I'm dedicated to solving crimes, and I believe that I do it well. The toughest part is always telling the family. It's a hard moment, just like all those times when you have to ask them questions. But, at the same time, they know that you're looking for justice on behalf of their loved ones."

"And now?"

"Well, it's a different case, but I wanted to ask you a question. How did you feel when your great-nephew arrived and then later when he betrayed you? I know that you've told me before."

"Look, Detective, blood is blood. I didn't have any relatives left in the world, and actually he was a joy."

"Do you think it would've been the same if you'd been married or if you'd had kids?"

Del Roble thought about it for a few moments.

"I don't know, but I think so. There's a difference between the family that one raises, and the ties one has with parents and siblings, especially if they're already dead and forgotten. My mother always said that, and I didn't understand her back then."

"And when you learned that he'd betrayed you?"

"I already told you that I forgave him a long time ago, in part because it's hard to be angry with the dead and because pleasant memories linked me to him, and also because I thought he was good and the circumstances led him to behave in a way that was untrue to himself."

Maria slept more peacefully that night. She kept clinging to the phrase "blood is blood." The first thing the next morning, even before Fernandez arrived, she went to see Keppler, brought him up to date on the investigation, and told him that she and her colleague needed to go to Tampa because it was too delicate a matter to be placed in the hands of the local police who were unfamiliar with the case.

"We can go by car if the budget is a problem. Larry, I want to solve this before the end of the year."

Keppler authorized them to fly and to rent a car in Tampa.

"Be careful, *Mariita*, it's a complicated situation," her boss advised.

When Fernandez arrived, she brought him up to date. They needed to think about what would be the best time to knock on Alexis's door and whether they wanted her husband to be home or not. She had already confirmed that the young woman worked as a teacher at a high school and that she usually dropped off and picked up her daughter at a house where a woman took care of her in the afternoons. They tended to get home around four in the afternoon. Her husband worked at a real estate firm and didn't have a fixed schedule, but he was usually home by six or six thirty, although sometimes he'd go back out.

The plane took off at noon, and by four thirty in the afternoon, they were knocking on the door of the young woman who might be Gladys Elena Lazo's missing baby.

The woman didn't open the door until they showed her their police badges. They assured her she didn't have anything to fear, that they just wanted to ask her a few questions. They maintained a professional yet friendly tone.

She finally let them in. Maria immediately realized that they were not dealing with the girl they were searching for. She didn't look anything like her, and she was a little older.

"Are you Alexis Smith, married to Nicholas, and do you have
a daughter?"

"No. Why do you ask?"

"Do you know them?"

"No, and I've never heard their names."

"Does a couple with a young daughter live on this street?"

"There are a lot of young families who live in the neighborhood, but I
don't know many people. I just moved here recently with my mother."

"And who did you buy the house from?"

"Look, why don't you tell me what this is about?"

"It's complicated…we won't ask you any more questions. Only who were
the previous owners?"

"An older couple. He died and the lady wanted to live in a smaller place,
in one of those retirement communities."

"Did you meet her? About how old was she?"

"Yes, I met her on the day of the closing. She must have been
about eighty."

Maria and Fernandez left the house deflated and greatly disillusioned.
They were convinced that they had found the baby who had been
missing for twenty-three years, but the lead that seemed to have been so
sure turned out to be false.

They returned to the hotel devastated. They felt like everything they had
worked for had been in vain. Where had they gone wrong? They spent
the rest of the evening speculating where they had made a mistake and
how all the doors could have possibly slammed closed.

They had a drink at the hotel bar. Maria could only eat a bowl of soup.
She felt a lump in her throat, a great sense of frustration.

"What are we going to do now?"

The question was as much for Fernandez as it was for her.

"Sleep," her colleague answered with pragmatism. "In the morning maybe we'll see things more clearly," he said to cheer her up.

Maria hardly slept a wink. She felt that same typical uneasiness associated with being on the brink of solving a case. It seemed absurd because she felt more lost now than when she had opened those two boxes in the station conference room about a month or so ago.

Chapter 27

Day 37—Tuesday, December 8, 2015

By eight o'clock in the morning, Maria had showered and dressed. She went to turn on her laptop and realized that she hadn't charged it. She was about to call Fernandez when he knocked on the door to her room. He had two Starbucks lattes. Maria almost hugged him.

"Do you have your iPad?"

Fernandez took it out of his briefcase.

"Do another search for Nicholas and Alexis's property in Tampa."

A few minutes later, they discovered their mistake. Maria had copied down the wrong address, the one on the line right below the Smiths' property. Both were from Tampa, but in different neighborhoods.

The day seemed excruciatingly long waiting for four o'clock to roll around so they could head down to the couple's house, and this time they were a lot more anxious.

When a woman opened the door, neither Fernandez nor Duquesne had any doubt. She looked so much like Elena Lozano that it was impossible for them not to be sisters.

They identified themselves, and, without letting them in, she told them that it would be better if they returned when her husband was home.

That's when Maria spoke to her in Spanish.

"It's related to your mother, who we know died a few years ago…"

Alexis opened the door and gestured for them to have a seat. She offered them water, a soda, or lemonade, but they didn't want anything. *Just like her mother, polite…* Maria thought. She could tell Alexis was nervous and thought that accepting something to drink might give her a second to gather herself, so Maria said:

"Actually, if it isn't too much trouble, I think I would appreciate something to drink and you probably would too, right Fernandez?"

They waited quietly, looking around at the place while the young woman prepared the drinks in the kitchen. Maria saw the graduation picture with her daughter who must have been about three or four at the time. She also saw a wedding picture of the young woman, but none of Soledad.

When all three were seated, Maria began speaking in English. She thought it was the more neutral language and the easiest one for all three of them to hide their emotions.

"So, your mother's name has surfaced in an investigation, and there are a few things that remain unclear, and we think you can help us with that. Soledad has already passed away and no harm can come to her, nor you, but you could help us solve a different case."

"When you were young, did you live in the New York area?"

"Yes, when I was very little. I wasn't even in school yet."

"And that's where your father died?"

Alexis seemed a bit unsettled.

"Yes, in an accident. I don't remember much about him. Like I said, I was pretty young."

"But your name wasn't Alexis back then, it was Soledad. Why did you change your name?"

The woman appeared more and more nervous.

"My name was Soledad Alexandra, but everyone called me Alexis. When I got married, I took my husband's last name, and I also took the opportunity to change my first name to the one everyone called me anyway."

"Did your mother tell you anything before she died?"

"Of course, she told me many things. I don't know what you mean."

"If she told you anything about your life that you didn't know, anything about your birth…"

Alexis looked like she was about to burst into tears.

Finally, in a quivering voice, she said:

"She told me she wasn't my birth mother, that I was adopted."

"And that's all?"

"Yes…"

"And have you tried to look for your real mother?"

"I've thought about that many times, but I haven't made up my mind."

"Why?"

"Because my mother was very good to me. She loved me a lot. She lived for me."

"If she told you before she died that you were adopted, maybe she wanted you to look for your parents. Don't you think?"

"Yes…maybe…well…"

"We can help you."

The young woman raised her gaze that had been glued to the floor up to now and asked in a shaky voice:

"Do you know who she is? Is she looking for me?"

Maria wasn't sure what to say, but Fernandez knew it was better not to rush it.

"No, we don't know, but we have access to many cases of women looking for their children after they gave them up for adoption…or, in some cases, some children are missing or kidnapped."

Alexis protested.

"That is not the case with me. My mother did not kidnap me. She saved my life…"

"So then, you know the circumstances…"

"No…"

"Look, Sole…sorry, Alexis… We don't want to upset you."

Maria had intentionally used the name that she went by when she was young. It worked. The young woman burst into tears.

Duquesne and Fernandez let her cry. Maria pushed the glass of water that Alexis had hardly touched closer to her.

"It's ok. Have some water. She died, and you two loved each other very much. Nothing that you tell us can harm her now."

"I just don't want to spoil her memory or tarnish the image I have of her. I assure you that she was a great mother."

"Did she leave a letter, or any other document to be read after her death?"

Alexis hesitated. A few seconds later, she said:

"Yes, before she died she asked me to forgive her… I assured her that there was nothing to forgive. That's when she confessed to me that I was adopted, she asked me not to judge her, and she said that she had done it to save my life…"

"And the letter?"

"She said it was in a safe here in Tampa, but she hoped I would wait for five years after her death to read it."

"And have you read it?"

"I haven't dared. Besides, it's just recently been five years. My husband says it's my decision, but that I should read it, that she wouldn't have left it if she didn't want me to know what it says. But it scares me…"

"Why?"

"Because I always sensed that my mother hid many secrets from me, but I never wanted to ask…and now…now I'm afraid."

That's when they heard keys in the door, and a tall, handsome man entered. At that second a little voice yelled:

"Daddy's home!" and a little girl, about five years old, ran to greet him and threw her arms around his neck. The man held her and looked at the detectives, rather unsurprised. Alexis introduced them.

"I knew at some point you would come," Nicholas Smith said to them.

Maria and Fernandez gave each of them their card and stood up to leave.

"Look, you two talk things over. We're going to be in Tampa for a short time, and we have to get this cleared up. It would be good if you decided to read the letter. Can we come back at this same time tomorrow or at another time that works for you?"

Mr. Smith walked them out. When he said goodbye, he told them:

"Come back tomorrow night at eight. We will have eaten dinner by then, and our daughter will be asleep. We'll try to clear everything up then. That will be best thing for my wife."

Chapter 28

Days 37 and 38—Tuesday and Wednesday, December 8 and 9, 2015

Maria let Fernandez drive. She was a little nervous driving in unfamiliar cities while also paying attention to the GPS, which indicated the correct lane to be in and where to turn, especially if she wanted to think clearly. She knew that they had finally found the lost child that they had spent over a month looking for and that had consumed her birth mother for decades. In large part, their case was already resolved, but she also wanted to know the story of what had happened during the past twenty-three years and, above all, to try to ease the trauma of their reunion as much as possible.

She was so engrossed in her thoughts that Fernandez had to ask her twice:

"Have you been to Ybor City before?"

"Honestly, no…"

"Then we'll take advantage of the time we have because there's a lot to see. How are you on money?"

"The same as always."

"Would you like to splurge a bit and go to the oldest Spanish restaurant in the city? Don't even try to object. It's not like the ones in Miami."

Maria hesitated.

"Come on, you've taught me that when you get some distance from your problems, that's when things surface and come to light more quickly… Let's not think about the case tonight. There's nothing we can do until we go to the Smiths' house tomorrow."

They stopped by the hotel so that Maria could change clothes and, a half hour later, they met in the lobby. With his characteristic efficiency, Fernandez had made a reservation at Columbia's, founded in 1905 by Casimiro, a Cuban. The establishment had stayed in the family for five generations, in good times and bad. Now, it was in a magnificent Spanish-style mansion, with a fountain in a central patio around which were some twenty tables as well as private dining rooms. The temperature was still pleasant outside in early December so they chose a table on the patio.

"Do you prefer a mojito or a daiquiri? They're both excellent here."

Maria had thought she would order a glass of wine but the enthusiasm in her partner's voice made her change her mind.

"Whatever you recommend."

"Let's get a pitcher of mojitos. They're exquisite here with real mint. They're as good, if not better, than the ones from Bodeguita del Medio. At least, that's what I've been told."

Maria ended up letting Fernandez choose what they would eat. They brought her the best tasting garbanzo bean soup that she had ever eaten in her life and later they shared three *tapas*: one of garlic shrimp; another of *piquillo* peppers stuffed with mushrooms, *chorizo*, and *jamón serrano* covered with Manchego cheese; and then chicken croquets that were even better than her grandmother's. As they savored the delicacies and the second pitcher of mojitos, their conversation became more animated. They talked about Jose Marti and his relationship to the cigar factories in Ybor City, their favorite restaurants in Miami, and their favorite music. Not once did they mention anything about the case or their work. Maria was impressed more and more by Fernandez's knowledge and expertise. She had never paid much attention to him before he had been randomly chosen to help her. She felt bad about that and promised herself that she would get to know the younger people in the department better.

When they came by with the dessert menu, Maria was certain she couldn't eat another bite, but Fernandez insisted that she try the mango mousse pastry.

The first taste took her back to her childhood; her parents would take her to the beach on Sundays in the summer and her mother would always pack mangos with their lunch. She loved to eat them and let the juice drip down her chin before wading into the water to rinse it off. One time she saw her father slurp up the golden juice with a kiss, just at the point where her mother's bathing suit covered her breasts. She had felt a little bit of embarrassment mixed with jealousy. Afterwards, whenever her mother offered her a mango, she gladly accepted it and, years later, as she had learned from her mother, she continued to savor the sweet tropical fruit by the sea.

The whole thing brought back such a vivid memory of her mother that she thought she might break down with one of those unexpected crying fits, but it soon occurred to her that she was in the process of returning a lost daughter to her family, and her mother would be glad to know that she had solved the case.

Fernandez asked for the check. They both took out their credit cards and split the bill. They left in silence. Maria suddenly felt a chill. She had the strange feeling that something important was about to happen. She knew that her work as a detective was based on thorough investigation more than anything else, but there was also a part that was pure intuition. And something was up.

Instinctively, she looked at her phone even though she hadn't heard it ring during dinner. In fact, she had a short message.

"Let me know where I can meet you two tomorrow at eight in the morning."

It was from Nicholas Smith, the husband of Gladys Mercedes/Soledad Alexandra/Alexis.

Maria replied and asked him if he would like to eat breakfast with them in the hotel. He accepted immediately.

Detective Duquesne couldn't fall asleep. Between having eaten a larger dinner than she was used to and the curiosity about what Smith was going to tell them in the morning, she tossed and turned in the bed, but never managed to drift off. She tried to read, play Solitaire on her phone, and watch TV. She wanted to call her dad, but didn't want to wake him and startle him at that hour. It wasn't until after three o'clock in the morning that she finally managed to fall asleep.

Although she barely got any rest, the next morning she felt refreshed after a shower, a cup of coffee, and with the expectation of their upcoming visit. Before eight o'clock, Fernandez and Maria were waiting anxiously in the lobby.

They finally saw Smith arrive. After exchanging the obligatory greetings, they sat down at the most private table they could find in the hotel restaurant.

"I'd rather order à la carte than eat from the buffet," Maria said with the hope that the rest would do the same to avoid everyone getting up for food repeatedly from the buffet.

All three chose the continental breakfast of orange juice, coffee, and a small basket of rolls.

The detectives didn't want to pressure their visitor although they were both anxious to hear what he had to say.

After his first cup of coffee, he finally began to speak.

"So, I wanted to see you before tonight because I want this issue to be as painless for my wife as possible. She's already suffered enough."

"We want the same for her," Maria assured him.

"You've found her parents?"

Maria hesitated, but was frank.

"We think so, but we can't confirm it without a DNA test. Do you have any information that might help us?"

"Alexis and I both lived in Tampa, but ironically we didn't meet until the summer before she left for Notre Dame. I was in my second year there, and I was back in Tampa on break. We fell madly in love. Not long afterwards, her mother became ill. It was pancreatic cancer, and we knew from the start that it was terminal and, in fact, she barely lived for a couple of more months. Soledad and I got along well, and it comforted her to know that she wasn't leaving her daughter behind and alone. One day, she whispered to me that she wanted to talk to me, that she needed to see me by myself. They had already decided to take her to hospice, but she asked them to wait until I got there, and she had even refused the morphine that would have helped with the discomfort. The cancer had spread to her bones, and she was in a great deal of pain."

Smith paused to finish his coffee.

"She struggled to speak, but she told me what she loved most in her life was her daughter. I nodded and told her not to worry about trying to say anything, and that I promised I'd take good care of her, but she needed to tell me something. She told me that Sole—that's what she always called her in private—was not her daughter. Two days before, right in front of me, she had told her that she was adopted. My wife didn't seem too surprised by that, and she assured her that she had been the best mother in the world and that she had no other mother besides her. But her mother told more of the story."

Smith refilled his coffee cup, added cream to it, and stirred it slowly as if buying time to choose the right words.

"She told me that she had stolen her daughter when she was a baby. 'It was to save her life' she repeated over and over. I couldn't get over my astonishment. I knew that the woman was dying and didn't want to go to her grave with such a secret. She then told me that she had written a letter to her daughter a couple of months before when she had been diagnosed with cancer. She entrusted me with where she had hidden it, and asked me to give it to Alexis once I felt that she could grasp what she had confessed and forgive her. I told her that in order to be able to do that, I would need to read the letter first. She gave me permission to do so, but not before I swore to her that I wouldn't share its contents with anyone."

Maria and Fernandez hung on every word that the man uttered. She knew that the letter held the answers to their investigation. Smith continued.

"I didn't want to read it until after the funeral. I read it several times and kept it in a safe deposit box in a bank. I still didn't think Maria was ready to know the truth, and, shortly after we got married, she got pregnant with our daughter. We hadn't planned on it, imagine, with us both studying, but we love her very much and she helped Alexis get through her depression after the death of her mother. Still, sometimes Alexis would complain about how her mother had left her with so many unanswered questions. Finally, I let her know about the letter, but I lied and told her that her mother requested that she wait five years before she read it. I also didn't tell her that I had read it. Yesterday, when she went to the kitchen to get you water, she called me and told me that you were there. Truthfully, I was waiting for the police to come eventually. So, I ran to the bank before it closed and took out the letter and made three copies of it. Last night, after you left, I gave the original copy to my wife. Alexis hasn't been able to take it all in yet, and she couldn't bring herself to go to work. She never misses work... I just left our daughter at daycare and the woman who takes care of her in the afternoons is going to pick her up later. When we're done here, I'll go back to Alexis and I'll call you later to tell you if she is in a state where she can speak to you this evening. However, I've brought two copies of the letter so that you can read it, but on one condition."

"What's that?"

"I want you to read it in front of me and then return it to me. You can't copy it, photograph it, or take notes. When you see my wife, only she can authorize whether or not you can have a copy of the letter."

The detectives agreed. They left the restaurant and sat in the comfortable lobby, quite empty at mid-morning. Smith gave them each an envelope, and they both began to read Soledad's letter written to the daughter she had raised.

Chapter 29

Day 38—Wednesday, December 9, 2015

Beloved Mija:

I don't know if I have the right to call you mija. *The first thing I ask is that you not judge me and that you don't hate me. You are the person that I've loved most in my life, but I have probably hurt you a lot, I don't know. I've wanted to tell you these things many times. I was afraid you'd reject me, that I'd lose you, that you wouldn't understand me and I always kept putting it off for later. Now that I am sick with cancer and I am going to die, I still don't have the courage to tell you things face to face so I'm writing them to you, even though I don't know how to do it so that you will read it at the best moment, or whether it's even possible for there to be a good moment to learn about so many secrets.*

Where to begin? I suppose at the beginning. My mother was a prostitute. I was born in Puerto Rico. I never knew who my father was. I don't think that she did either, and she didn't even get me a birth certificate. So legally, I didn't exist. She wasn't bad to me. In her own way, she loved me. She was completely uneducated. She didn't know how to read or write, but I went to a little neighborhood school and I learned. From that point on, I was helpful to her with many things and I think that's why she was acting better with me. What I mean is, now and then she would give me a peseta for lunch or she would buy me a toy for my birthday or for All King's Day. I became a woman or rather I got my first period at about twelve years old. I began to develop and the men who visited her would look me up and down. She would immediately send me to some neighbor's house. She never allowed one of those guys to lay a hand on me. But there was one who wouldn't give up. One night when she thought I was asleep, I heard them talking. He offered her a large sum of money, I think about five thousand dollars, which at that time—and for my mother—was a fortune, and he promised her that he would marry me and treat me like a queen.

I was fifteen years old! I was very scared, but I was sure that the guy was drunk and that my mother wasn't really going to sell me. I fell asleep. The next morning she was more affectionate than ever with me and I felt happy. I thought that this man's proposal had made her realize that she loved me...she even came to pick me up from school that afternoon and she bought me a new dress. That evening, for the first time that I ever remember, she kissed me goodnight.

I don't know what happened next. They must have given me some type of drug, because when I woke up I was in a shitty hotel. I began to scream and yell for my mother. She never came. The truth is, I never saw her again or even heard anything else about her. Instead, the scumbag that had bought me for five thousand dollars was there. That same morning he raped me. I was a virgin and I think that's what attracted him. He fed me well, he didn't hit me or say ugly things, but when he had sex with me I was repulsed. In the days that followed, other girls arrived, all young and virgins, and some days he'd leave me alone, although later he took to having us girls fondle each other and kiss each other on the mouth while he watched and masturbated. In short, I don't want to give you any more details about that period of my life that was so brutal and yet, somehow, managed to get even worse.

When there got to be about five, six, or seven young girls—I don't remember how many—he took us to New York. It never occurred to me to think about how he got me papers. In order to travel he got me an ID that even had my picture. I didn't know anything about those things back then. Eventually we got to a house with many rooms, decorated with flashy colors, some red, others violet, with a big lounge and a bar. That's where the Madame met us, gave us provocative clothing, and a series of lessons and warnings. So basically, that lowlife had purchased us in order to exploit us as prostitutes. At first, I suffered a lot, and I even thought that the guy had stolen me and that my mother would come rescue me, but eventually you get used to it... In the worst moments, I would think about the beaches in Puerto Rico...Luquillo...Isla Verde...so pretty... But not everything was all bad. The girls and I made friends, especially the Hispanics, because there were also Asians who would hang out separately.

After sleeping in the mornings, we would talk in the afternoons, and we would cry and laugh together. We even planned how we would escape.

I don't know how much time went by. Maybe two years, maybe three. I know that I was no longer an adolescent but a young woman. One client that they called "El Oso" started showing up. They said he was a womanizer, that he liked them all, but, after being with me twice, he wasn't with any of the other girls ever again. He was a little gruff, but he didn't treat me badly, and since he knew they didn't give me hardly any cash, sometimes he'd bring me a little gift—chocolates, some perfume—or he'd give me a small bill and say, "Hide this well. This is just for you."

The truth is that I didn't have any way to spend it because they rarely let us out. One day El Oso kept looking at me and told me: "Wait, I know who you are."

I didn't remember having seen him before I went to Madame's house but after a few weeks, one day he remembered: "Didn't you used to live in Puerto Rico?"

It turned out that he worked as an expert in falsifying documents, and he was the one that had made the papers for us girls when the guy bought us, and, from that time on, I was certain that's what had happened.

Well, I don't know if El Oso was capable of falling in love, but he was growing fond of me and, why would I lie to you, I felt the same. I don't know what kind of deal he made with the owner of the place or with the Madame, but one night he brought me a dress and some shoes and said, "Get dressed, you're getting out of here."

Within a few days we moved to Miami. The early days weren't bad. He concentrated on his scams, I took care of the house—well, trailer—where we lived, and I can tell you that compared to the earlier years of my life, this part was almost happy. I really wanted to have a child, but he refused, saying that we had to travel light, that he wasn't a family man, and that I shouldn't get my hopes up.

I admit that I tricked him. You know that us women have a way of arranging those things. Finally I got pregnant. I thought that now in that situation he'd be happy or, at least, he'd accept it. None of that. He got pissed and took me almost by force to a clinic where they gave me such a back alley abortion that later I wound up with a terrible infection. I thought I was going to die. One night a neighbor lady saw me so badly off that she called 911. They had to do an emergency operation. They said that after that I would never be able to have children.

I'm telling you these things that I'd like to forget and had hoped you'd never find out because my wish is that they'll make you understand better what happened later. I became very depressed. Nothing mattered to me. Even he didn't care to fight with me like before. At night, he'd get cleaned up and he'd go out alone. Shortly thereafter the incidents at the Peruvian Embassy in Havana took place and Cubans started leaving through Mariel. That's when I found out that he was from Cuba because up until then I'd believed he was Boricua, *although I don't know why I thought he was from Puerto Rico, since he didn't talk like me.*

One day he told me that we were going to work together and make a lot of money. I froze. I thought he was going to force me back into prostitution and I couldn't have handled it. But that wasn't the case. He took me with him to Tamiami Park, where there were many refugees and a lot of confusion. He told me my job was to get close to the families and to make friends with the children and the women, and to find out what worried them the most. Then I was supposed to report back to him and then introduce him to the ones he chose. I could write a book about the stories I heard, but El Oso only wanted to meet the people that had something to hide or needed some document they'd not been able to bring with them. So I'd gain their confidence, and he'd falsify their documents. Many didn't have any way to pay him, but he got their relatives to do it. When they didn't have any family, he always said: "Don't worry about it, chico, *we'll figure out a way for you to pay me later."*

The truth is, some of them benefitted from the situation and settled up with him. When they finally closed Tamiami Park, we left for Fort Chaffee. I don't know how he snuck in so that we could work there as volunteers but soon we were doing the same thing. It was harder there because few had relatives in the United States or they hadn't been able to locate them, but he was able to gather information from reports. Those refugees assimilated to life in the United States and, in one way or another, he would collect.

Now, mijita, *here comes the hardest part where you and your father come in. His name was Alberto Gonzalez and he came to the United States through Mariel at age seventeen. However, in order to get out of Tamiami without problems, you needed to be eighteen. El Oso assured him that he could arrange it, and your father, who was just a kid, not suspecting anything, was thrilled. He got him a birth certificate, which showed him one or two years older and a social security number belonging to a man who had died. Later it turned out that your father found a great uncle who got him out of there and gave him a job. Maybe he wouldn't have needed those papers and his life would've been different, if he had found him earlier...*

Truth be told, with that art of falsifying documents and the quantity of people who came through Mariel, we lived well for a few years. But that had its limits. I thought that El Oso would also be able to do the same thing with, for example, the Nicaraguans, but somehow it was harder for him to falsify their documents, and that didn't work out. Later I thought that he might have some connections with the Cuban government... I couldn't believe that he was even able to get a Marielito writer a copy of his novel that the Cuban State Security forces had confiscated. Maybe he was even one of Castro's agents, but at that time it didn't occur to me.

As he earned less, he became nastier. The truth is he was flat broke. I was already pretty resentful of him because he forced me to get an abortion and it was his fault that I couldn't have kids, but the thing is that he'd never really valued me just for who I was. My documents were false and I didn't know how to escape. So I began watching him work with the idea that one day I could make my own papers and begin a new life.

It was in that period that El Oso began blackmailing those who'd never paid him. Even if they had paid, they were living with false documents

that could get them deported to Cuba if they were discovered by
Immigration, or at least that's what he told them.   ˋ

Among others, he began taking money from your father. Alberto was
a good man, and, since he didn't want to cause problems for his great
uncle who had hired him, he started paying. At first, El Oso asked him
for small sums and we'd meet up in a store in Miami Beach, and he'd give
him the cash.

But El Oso was bad, and he knew how to squeeze people. He kept asking
Alberto to help him rob his great uncle's business. He refused for months
until the pressure was so severe that he caved. It was obvious that your
father felt very bad about betraying the very person who had helped him,
but El Oso kept pressing him to rob his uncle's house, in addition to the
business. Your father moved from there and hid from us a while. I felt
ashamed and I told El Oso to leave him alone, that there was no use
beating a dead horse. He threatened him so much that Alberto gave in.
Your father assured him that it was the last time because he didn't have
anything else to give him. The truth is that the whole thing was really ugly
because even the poor old man wound up beaten.

For some time, I think for about a year, Alberto stayed somewhat
underground and El Oso found other victims and left him alone for a
while. One day, I don't remember how, we found out that Alberto had
gotten married and he'd just had a son...or a daughter.

"When you have a family, you do anything to protect it. This guy isn't
going to want them finding out that he's been using a false social security
number for twelve years. He could go to jail," El Oso said.

Finally he found him. Then came Hurricane Andrew. I insisted that
El Oso leave him alone because the poor guy didn't have a penny
to his name.

"Everybody has something," he said.

He arranged to meet him a few days after Andrew near the house where
we lived at the time near Krome Avenue. Your father brought two hundred

dollars and said: "This is all I have. I beg you to leave me alone or I'm going to turn you in to the police. I don't care anymore what happens to me. I have a wife and a daughter now. I can't keep living like this."

They got into it. El Oso punched him and Alberto fell backwards and hit his head on a brick. At least that's what El Oso told me because I was inside the house and I didn't see it. He put him in the car that Alberto had driven and he came running into the house, gave me the keys and said: "Come on, run, follow me."

I followed him to a grassy area near a canal. I saw that he put Alberto in the driver's seat and put it in drive so it would go into the canal. But it didn't move. He called me over to help him.

When I got closer, I saw that there was a bag and a car seat in the back. Without thinking, in the blink of an eye, I opened the door, removed the bag, and I saw you. I don't know how I was able to unbuckle the little seatbelt that was holding you. Then the car started moving forward. I threw myself on the ground with you and the bag between my arms. I heard El Oso close the door just before it fell into the water, and he yelled at me: "Holy shit, Soledad. What have you done?"

Chapter 30

Day 38—Wednesday, December 9, 2015

"Excuse me," Maria told Smith breaking the absolute silence that the three of them had shared. "I have to go to the ladies' room for a second and need a bottle of water." She handed him the letter.

"Hang on to this while I go."

"No problem. I'll go get us some water."

Like Maria, Fernandez took advantage of the moment to stretch and go to the restroom. He crossed paths with her on the way, but they didn't speak. The mysteries were becoming clear, and many of the things they'd learned were being confirmed, but reading it in the words of a woman condemned to death in some way added a human element that was very different from the cold police reports.

Moments later, without so much as a word spoken among the three of them, Smith handed them the papers again. This second part began with different colored ink.

Beloved Mijita, *I had to stop writing for a few days. You know how depressed I get after those treatments. Sometimes, I feel like I'd rather die, and I'm not exaggerating because I know that's going to happen anyway. I think that you'll be more at peace if you think that you've done everything possible to save me, at least until you read this confession. I know your kindness and your love for me and that's why it scares me so much to write all of this down for you. I keep writing, not knowing whether I'll tear up this letter in the end, but I think that at least I owe you the truth, even if you hate me for the rest of your life. I would deserve it.*

So, let's get back to where I was in this long and tangled story of our lives together. El Oso *went crazy when I took you out of the car. He tried to snatch you out of my arms and throw you into the canal. I was holding*

*you tight and told him not to be stupid, that if he did, you'd float up and
they'd discover the crime.*

*"Ok, then we'll go get some weights to put on her... Have you gone nuts?"
he yelled.*

*I told him that it was his fault that I couldn't have children and asked him
to let me raise you. I thought we could be a family. You were crying, and
he was afraid we'd attract attention. He tried to rip you from my arms.
Look, I am not very religious, but if there are miracles, at that moment
God worked one. You stopped crying and, just like that, the tiny little thing
that you were, maybe not even a month old, you smiled at him and that
very bad man's heart melted. I knew that we had won the battle when he
pushed me toward the car saying, "Ok, let's go home and we'll see."*

*We didn't stay in Miami very long out of fear that they'd discover us. We
drove almost nonstop the whole way to New Jersey where he had friends. I
bought you diapers, bottles, milk, and a few clothes. I'd never taken care of
a baby. You were a little angel. You drank up all the milk, the orange juice,
and you hardly ever cried. I had to work extra hard to tend to El Oso to
keep him from getting jealous. I also didn't want you to bother him. He
didn't seem to show much interest, but he never spoke again about us
getting rid of you and once, when he thought I wasn't watching, he went
up to you and smiled. If there was anything good in that man, I only saw
it in his eyes when he looked at you.*

*You were probably about six months old when he came home with
some papers.*

*"Check it out. I've made the baby a birth certificate. Someday she'll have
to go to school, and she'll need it," he said.*

*I breathed easily from that time on. There were some pretty good times.
El Oso was no longer living from falsifying documents. Instead, he was
selling drugs. I knew that it was wrong, but I tried not to think about
that. You were my world. And I enjoyed watching you grow, your first
tooth, your first words, your first steps, and the delight with which you ate
bananas, which you loved. I begged him not to ever bring drugs home, and*

I'm almost sure that he listened to me. At least, I never saw anything in that tiny little apartment that we had in Queens.

I think you were about a year and a half old, more or less, when one day, all of a sudden, he told me that things weren't going well, and I needed to get a job. No matter how many times I asked, he never spoke frankly; everything was a constant fight. He gave me a piece of paper with a name and address.

"Look, this friend of mine has a factory and he's looking for help," he said.

"But I don't know how to do anything," I explained.

He insisted: "You're smart. They'll teach you."

I kept resisting: "Look genius, and the baby?"

"She's bigger now. We'll find someone to take care of her," he replied.

My objections fell on deaf ears. Besides, I thought that as soon as they saw that I didn't have any work experience, they weren't going to hire me. I was wrong. Now I think that he had it all arranged. Besides, I didn't think that things were going so badly for him, and the little bit that I was going to make there wasn't going to help us much.

Those were hard years, especially the winters. I would get up early to take you to Odalys's house, a marvelous woman who grew very fond of you. Then I'd take I don't know how many trains or buses to get to the factory. There I was, sitting for eight hours in front of a sewing machine. They barely gave us a fifteen-minute break in the mornings, and fifteen in the afternoon, and thirty for lunch. Only two good things happened during those days. I made very good friends and, with what I learned, I began making you some adorable outfits. I even dreamed that someday I'd make your wedding gown.

Now, I think that my love for you made me egotistical. I never thought about your real mother or how much she must've suffered thinking that you had drowned in the canal. I felt like your savior and your mother, and I didn't allow anything to get in my way.

Not too many months had gone by before the boss started sending me on errands that struck me as odd. Sometimes he'd call me to the office and say, "Soledad, when you come this way tomorrow, would you mind stopping for a second at the bodega on the corner? They're going to give you a package for me. Stick it in your purse and bring it to me when you get here."

Since I must've had a surprised look on my face, he added: "They're some special threads that I ordered."

Each time the errands became more frequent and occasionally I had to switch trains or buses.

"Don't worry if you get here a little late," he said to calm me down.

The other girls, however, didn't like that sometimes I clocked in an hour later even though, as far as I knew, they weren't aware of the boss's errands or that they weren't deducting that time from my pay. Actually, they'd raised my salary.

El Oso *was on cloud nine. On Sundays, the three of us would go out and there were moments when it seemed like we were just like any other family. At times I felt nervous although I didn't understand exactly the mess that I was getting into.*

I found out a few weeks later. On one of our Sunday outings, seemingly by chance, we ran into the owner of a little shop where I'd pick up packages frequently for the boss. He and El Oso *greeted each other with an embrace. It was all very fast and I wouldn't have suspected anything if it hadn't had been that all of a sudden I realized that you had a doll in your hands that I'd never seen before. I figured that you'd taken it from another girl in the park, although you usually didn't do things like that. I scolded you and you began crying.* El Oso *intervened: "Come on, Soledad, leave the poor girl alone."*

When you calmed down and stopped crying, you looked at me with those big beautiful eyes of yours and said, "I didn't steal the doll, Mami. El Oso's

friend gave it to me." You called him that because he never wanted you to
call him Papá.

"Of course, Soledad, that guy is one of my pals. Don't give the girl a hard
time," he said, defending you.

I felt a shiver go down my spine. There was something fishy going on.
Immediately the sunny Sunday turned gray. We returned home in silence.

Maybe I was wrong to confront him, I don't know. That night I asked him
to tell me the truth: what did he have to do with those packages that I
was picking up for the boss, who was that man we ran into, and why had
he given you a doll? At first he started ignoring me, paying me no mind,
until he finally explained: "I would have preferred that you didn't know
but since you're bugging me so much I'll tell you. I really don't know how
you didn't figure it out sooner. They're drugs, Soledad, and now you're up
to your ass deep in it with me so don't even think about going against me,
blabbing a word to anyone, or not doing what the boss says. Up to now
you've been pretty good."

I couldn't sleep a wink. How could I have been such a dumbass? My world
came crashing down. I, the one who lived to protect you, who worried
when you'd scrape a knee or if you didn't eat right on any given night,
had put the two of us in the middle of drug trafficking! Of course, nothing
would've happened to you, but if they had found out the truth about me,
I would've gone to jail. I would've had to tell the truth so they could've
found your real mother because I wasn't going to let them give you to
just any old family, and I figured I'd never get out of jail. Those thoughts
tormented me.

I swear I didn't plan it. It's true that there were moments when I wished El
Oso *would disappear from our lives, even that he'd die. At the same time,*
he was the only person that I had in my life, and our relationship wasn't
bad. In our own way, we loved each other. He didn't tell me everything
that he did and I didn't ask. We didn't live in luxury, but we also didn't
go without. How would you and I manage alone? I tried to think about
how we could get out, how to change our name now that I knew how to

falsify documents, and how to begin a new life where he wouldn't be able to find us.

Other times I knew that regardless of where we went, that bloodhound would find us for sure, even if we managed to escape. More and more the random meet ups when they would give you some toy became more frequent. "Who's going to suspect a little girl? The plan is sweet," he told me later with cynicism. I needed to save you from that kind of life, but I didn't know how.

One Sunday he woke up in a very good mood and told us to get dressed up nicely because we were going to catch the Staten Island Ferry to go meet a very nice family that had kids your same age. By now he'd already burned all bridges with me; I didn't believe anything that he told me, everything frightened me, but there wasn't a good enough excuse not to go.

It was a cold day. I don't remember the date, but you must've been about three years old. Maybe younger. I had dressed you in your prettiest little outfit, one that I had made for you from leftover swatches in the factory. It was made of wine-colored velvet with a little matching jacket. It's funny how we remember the most absurd things. On the walk there, El Oso gave you a lollipop. I was furious because I didn't like you eating at the wrong time, plus I feared that with the rocking of the ferry that you'd choke. We finally got to the house, which was very pretty and much more luxurious than any that I'd ever seen. There were lots of kids, so many that I didn't think they could all be from the same couple, because they were all more or less about the same age, between three and six. They were well dressed, clean, and had expensive toys, but there was something that I didn't like, but I couldn't put my finger on. We were sitting down snacking on some pastries, and you had sat down facing me, beside El Oso. At that moment, the man of the house got up to look for something and, before he returned to his seat, he stopped in front of you. He took your little face in his hands and gave you a kiss on the cheek that, to me, looked like it was on your lips. He turned around to your dad and said, with a devilish look: "She's an adorable girl. You should bring her around more often."

Sole, I felt like they had stuck a knife in the middle of my heart, like I was listening all over again to my mother talk to that lowlife that she sold me to for five thousand dollars. I knew that nothing good was going to come out of this. I had to go to the bathroom and throw up.

When we got back, it was already dark because in New York when they change the clocks it gets dark really early. Frankly, I didn't know what I was going to do, but there was no doubt that we had to get out.

As luck would have it just as we got to the dock, the ferry seemingly bumped into something and made a sharp movement. El Oso was beside me, leaning on the rail, looking at God knows what. He lost his balance and tried to hold on to me. I swear that I didn't plan it like this, it was just a survival instinct, but instead of helping him, I pushed him with all my might. Since we were the only ones on the deck, nobody saw me. Well at least I thought so but they did, however, notice that he went overboard. I prayed that he wouldn't make it out alive because if he did, he'd kill both of us, or at least me, and God knows what he would've done with you. We had to get out of there, but it was impossible right at that moment. Divers, police, and ambulances immediately arrived. May Heaven forgive me, but when they said that he was dead, I felt like a load was lifted off me. As much as I tried to avoid it, I had to give them our names, and they even took a picture of us and then we appeared in the newspapers. They told me that I could go to the morgue and identify the body and that in the morning we should go to the police station to fill out the paperwork. I heard someone say that I could get some money out of the company that operated the ferry.

I went home, packed our bags, and took every cent we had. I held you tight and told you everything would turn out ok and that you needed to be very brave. You consented with your big eyes that seemed even bigger since you were afraid. I drove until fatigue got the best of me. We stopped at a motel near the town of Valdese in North Carolina only for one night, but we stayed three years.

Chapter 31

Day 38—Wednesday, December 9, 2015

Maria was so focused on reading that it took her a few minutes to realize her cell was vibrating. When she saw that the call was from her boss, she answered immediately and moved a few steps away from the group so she could speak with him. She returned shortly thereafter and the frustration must have shown on her face because Fernandez asked:

"Is something wrong?"

"It was Keppler asking what time we're due to arrive because we have to be in court at nine in the morning for the Homestead case."

Detective Duquesne was doubly annoyed because there was no way to avoid returning to Miami and because, despite her jotting down everything in her agenda and adding reminders days in advance, she had completely forgotten about that unavoidable appearance in court. She knew that her testimony was important and that it was impossible for her to stay in Tampa.

"What'd you tell him?"

"That we would be there…well, after we see Alexis tonight. We can head out after that, even though we'll be beat when we get back."

"I can't promise you that she'll be ready to see you. Maybe it's better if you give her a little time to digest all this and then come back. Besides, everything is in this letter. She doesn't know anything else. What do you want from her?"

"Permission for a DNA test to prove her identity."

"Why the rush? Have you located her family?"

"We can't confirm that without the test."

Smith started gathering the papers.

"I should be with my wife. It's best if you guys return to Miami and I'll tell you when she's calmed down."

Fernandez was the one who asked:

"Do we have many pages left to finish the letter?"

Smith looked at his folder.

"No, there are just a few more."

Fernandez took a quick glance at his phone and looked at the two of them.

"There's a flight to Miami at a little after seven tonight. I can call the office so they'll book it for us. Meanwhile we can finish reading the letter. You can return to your wife in less than an hour, and, if you think that she'll agree to see us before we have to head out to the airport, we'll come by the house. And if that isn't the case, we'll stay in touch. You should help us convince her to agree to the test. One shouldn't go through life not knowing who you are…even if just for her own medical history and her daughter's."

As soon as Smith agreed with a nod, Fernandez contacted the departmental secretary to get them seats on the flight, and he went up to the registration desk to tell them that they'd be leaving in a few hours but they needed to vacate the rooms a little later than the noon checkout time. Since the hotel wasn't very full, and the truth is that hotel staff always treat the police with deference, they assured them that there wouldn't be a problem. With that settled, Smith gave them the third and final part of Soledad's letter to her daughter, written with still another different colored ink and handwriting that was shaky in the early paragraphs but became more legible as it progressed.

Forgive me, mijita, I had to interrupt this letter again. I'm going to try to be brief because I have very little strength and because I've already told you the worst. Let's see where I left off… I know. By pure coincidence we spent the first night near Valdese. I think it was because I was trying to avoid the highways in case they were looking for us and I was a little lost. Or maybe it was the work of God. The next morning we went to have breakfast in town with the intention of continuing on. I thought about heading to Miami since I knew it well but while I was sitting in a McDonald's with you, I realized that Miami would be the first place that they'd look for us and the only place I couldn't go. All of a sudden, I saw a sign that said, "Help wanted." I'd never worked in anything related to restaurants, but I was willing to do anything for you. The first thing I thought was, who's going to take care of Sole for me while I work? Where will we live? I asked to speak with the manager. It turned out that he was of Italian origin, like many in the town, where there were only two other Hispanic families. He suggested that I go to the church, where they helped the recent arrivals. They couldn't have been any nicer. In a few months we had rented an efficiency apartment in a big house with its own entrance. .   We had everything we needed. In the end, I didn't work for McDonald's. Instead, I cleaned the church, which wasn't Catholic, but it doesn't matter. They had a kind of daycare there where I left you during my work hours. When I had to work nights sometimes I would take you with me, and you would sit on the floor and color or read your books, as quiet as a mouse. Other times the pastor's wife, who was very fond of you, would offer to take care of you. I improved my English a lot since there wasn't anyone to speak Spanish to. I learned to crochet and made all kinds of placemats, coasters, and other things that sold in the annual bazaar in November. My customers liked them so much that throughout the year they placed orders with me. You seemed to flourish in such a healthy life. You started going to daycare and then first grade. Immediately you started reading. I wanted to achieve more so I could help you with your assignments, and I began checking out books from the library, and I even took home the newspapers that the pastor received, and I flipped through them to keep up to date with what was going on in the world and in town. Later an American woman wanted me to teach her Spanish, and she bought some books. I didn't know anything about accents or verbs or any of that, but with the book, I think I learned more than my student. I don't know how much you remember about those years which, for the two of us, were very happy. When you were six years old, they started little league soccer and you insisted that you play. I gave you everything you wanted that I could, and even some things that I couldn't, because in one way or another in that town, everyone helped one another. It was at that time that Mariela came on a school trip with her mother. They lived in the same building as the lady who took care of you when we lived in Queens. They were very happy to see us and said that Odalys missed you very much, asking how we could had left without saying goodbye or leaving a trace. You, with the innocence of a child, wanted Mariela to come home and play with you, and you told her that I worked at the church and the name of the school you attended. The truth is that I had never asked you to hide anything, nor had I falsified any documents to disguise us, because with a last name as common as Garcia and in that town that was so gringo and so small, I felt like nobody would ever find us.

I panicked and once again treated terribly everybody who had helped us because we took off like fugitives at first light. At least I left without owing anything, and I wrote a thank-you note saying that we were leaving due to a family emergency. I always wanted to take you back to that little town where we were so happy, but now you see it would have been impossible.

I headed south because I knew that life was easier where the winters weren't harsh. When we got to Florida and I studied the map, I don't know why I decided to go to Tampa. I wanted to be near the sea, and it seemed that on the west coast it would be harder for them to find us. That's when I told you the first big lie. Up to then I had hidden many things from you, but I had not lied. I made up a story about your birth registration being incorrect and now that we were moving, it was the best time to gather all of our papers. You were six or seven, so you didn't understand, plus those things just didn't matter to you. I didn't want to remove the name Soledad but I did add Alexandra. I thought the two of us would change our last name to Maldonado. It's pretty common in Puerto Rico, and I was convinced that they were looking for me as a Cuban. In the end, I kept Garcia, but changed other details. I made all the false documents before enrolling you in school, looking for a job, or getting a new driver's license. Also, I'm ashamed to say, I stole social security numbers for each of us. I knew it was fraud and for several months, I lived with the anxiety that they would find us out, but as time went on and nothing happened, I felt more confident. Besides, I never tried to get government benefits. I feared that if I had, they could investigate and find out the truth. I also told you that Soledad was a hard name for Americans, so it would be better for them to call you by your middle name, Alexandra, but I don't know if it was because it was too long or what, but you said that your name was Alexis and it stuck. I was the only one who kept calling you Sole. I swear that since then, I haven't broken any laws.

You already know the rest. At times, I worked up to three jobs so that you could have a childhood and an adolescence that were happy. I don't think you lacked anything, just the truth. My sacrifices paid off well. You always got good grades. There was never a complaint about you from the school. Your behavior and your attendance were perfect. You kept playing soccer and stood out. You won trophy after trophy! I never missed a game even though I had to beg to get a coworker to switch with me. The happiest day of my life was when you graduated with honors and told me that you had received a scholarship to study at Notre Dame. I thought my work was done and that it was time to tell you the truth. For the first time I began thinking about your family and it even occurred to me that you might have brothers and I thought about the danger of you meeting each other and falling in love. I had read about things like that. More than once I was about to tell you everything and I always lacked the courage.

You insisted that I move to Indiana with you, but I chose not to. I had my work and my life in Tampa. Only when they diagnosed me with cancer did I agree for you to bring me here, because I thought that it would be easier for you and because I wanted to be near you in my final days.

I like Nicholas a lot. I think you two were made for each other and I know that you're going to be very happy with him. I regret that I won't live to be by your side when you graduate from college or on your wedding day, that I won't be able to make your wedding dress as I once dreamed, and that I will never know my grandchildren.

Maybe when you're a mother you will understand me and forgive me or perhaps you'll hate me for the harm that I caused your real mother, who I don't know. I don't even know who she is, or I would tell you. I do know that you were born in Miami in August of 1992 and that your father's name was Alberto Gonzalez, although I think he used another name too. He came to the United States through Mariel, and now I remember that one time he referred to his wife as Gladys and he said she'd come from Cuba on a raft. Mija querida, *I ask again for your forgiveness for everything I've done and I hope that when you read this letter that you'll search for your mother. Because of me she didn't get to see you grow up and now I'm sorry even though you have been my whole life. I hope that you find her. When I am no longer here, repair the harm that I have done. Ask her to forgive me. I believe that's the only way I can rest in peace.*

I don't have much advice to give you. You are sensitive, smart, independent, and beautiful. You're going to go far in life. At least I can die peacefully knowing that I raised you well.

I love you very much, mi Sol,

Mami

Chapter 32

Days 38 and 39—Wednesday and Thursday, December 9 and 10, 2015

When they finished reading the letter, Maria and Fernandez gave it back to Smith, who placed the copies back in the original envelope. He immediately stood up and, as they were shaking hands, he said:

"You know this is off the record… I'll call you as soon as Alexis is calmer… I'm going to go be with her now."

"Nicholas…"

This was the first time Maria called him by his first name. He turned around and, as if he were reading her thoughts, said, "I agree with her mother, meaning Soledad, that she should look for her real mother. I'll try to convince her to let you do a DNA test. Give me a few days."

The detectives stood up quietly to gather their luggage and they met up at the counter to pay the bill.

"I already reconfirmed the flight. We still have a few hours. What do you know about Ybor City?"

"Only the stories my dad told me about how Marti would get the workers all riled up at the tobacco factories with his speeches and how they helped him with funds for the war in Cuba," Maria answered her colleague.

"Well, let's head over there. We aren't getting anything done sitting here."

"It's just that I…"

"Come on, Maria, stop racking your brains. The case is already solved and, as soon as the girl gives her permission, which she will, and her identification is proven, there will be a huge party in Hialeah."

"It isn't going to be that simple..."

"Whatever happens later, whether they hit it off or not, isn't part of our job anymore. In a few days we'll be slammed with other cases."

"I'll never forget this one."

"You're right about that, our investigations hardly ever have happy endings."

They talked while Fernandez drove to Ybor City, not far from the hotel. They had some Cuban sandwiches for lunch: maybe not as tasty as those from the famous Versailles restaurant in Miami, but not bad. The ham, cheese, and roasted pork were good quality. There were plenty of pickles, butter and mustard, and above all, the bread was delicious, and it was perfectly pressed and golden brown.

"Did you know that Cuban bread didn't come from Cuba but from here in Tampa?" Fernandez asked. Maria was no longer surprised by her colleague's varied knowledge. Fernandez told her something about a Spanish-Italian guy who had started a bakery in the city at the end of the nineteenth century, but she wasn't listening. She was enjoying lunch but kept thinking about how the meeting between the young woman and her family would go, because she was convinced that the DNA test was a formality and that the woman she had met yesterday was Gladys Elena Lazo's missing child.

The detectives visited the spot where Marti gave his famous speech, and they took pictures of each other posing as flowery orators. Fernandez told her how Ybor City and West Tampa used to be known as tobacco capitals, not just in the nineteenth century but also at the beginning of the twentieth. He also told her how they played *bolita*, an illegal crapshoot. Maria wasn't sure if that part was true or whether he was making it up just to amuse her, but, as her colleague sensed her doubts, he looked it up on his phone and showed it to her.

"See? I don't tell lies…well, not that kind."

They laughed, relieving the tension felt ever since they had read Soledad's letter. When they were finally at the airport gate waiting to board, Maria asked Fernandez whether she ought to call Smith.

"No" he answered emphatically. "Give them time."

She thought about how clever and useful her colleague had turned out to be in this case and how she would let the boss know. Maria arrived home after nine o'clock and immediately felt overcome with fatigue. She sent a message to her father, Patrick, and to David, telling them that she had gotten home but was exhausted so she would talk to them the following day.

At that moment, her phone rang and startled her.

"Forgive me, Duchess. You told me not to call you at this number unless it was an emergency, but…"

"Mercedes?"

"Yes, it's Mercy, the grandmother."

"What can I do for you?"

"Look, it isn't an emergency, but I need to see you."

"At this hour? I've just gotten home from a trip."

"From Tampa?"

This woman must be a witch or a detective, Maria thought. Without waiting for her to reply, the grandmother kept talking.

"No, not tonight. I know that you're tired right now. Whenever you can tomorrow."

"I have to be in court at nine. I don't know how long that will take. How about if I call you when it's over and I come by your house, unless you prefer to come to the station?"

"If you can come here, even better. I'm not going to work tomorrow. Stop by at whatever time you'd like. I'll be waiting for you."

Maria was intrigued by the call and remembered the grandmother's dream about the gray brick university, but she was so tired that she fell asleep the minute her head hit the pillow. The case for which she had to testify didn't begin until ten o'clock but it was one of the first ones called and they let her go by a quarter to eleven.

She got in touch with the station and her father to ensure that everything was ok, and she told Mercedes she would come by the house.

The first thing that surprised her when she arrived was a huge statue of Saint Lazarus in the front patio, which she didn't remember seeing before.

Mercy welcomed her with freshly brewed coffee and a warm hug.

"Come in, Duchess. Please sit down…over here so you're more comfortable."

Maria was already tired of correcting her that her last name was Duquesne and she had accepted the noble title that this quirky *pinareña* had bestowed upon her.

"Look, I'm going to get right to the point. I don't know how much you've figured out yet. Maybe it's a lot or maybe not that much, but regardless you can't say anything yet or you would've already told my daughter. I'm only going to share this with you: I am certain that my granddaughter is alive and that we're going to find her very soon. It is going to be a Saint Lazarus Day miracle."

"I appreciate the divine help."

"Don't be sarcastic, Duchess, because you aren't like that. Look, I'm going to tell you what happened to me. You've certainly heard of Saint

Lazarus, but I'm not sure if he's the same one that Christ brought back to life. I don't think so. In Cuba, his place of worship was near the leper colony. I'm sure you don't know what leprosy is because it doesn't exist anymore, but the sick would be all covered in sores, and it was very contagious. That's why they sent them to faraway places—maybe that's why they call the place with his altar 'El Rincon'—and the people that took care of them were considered true saints. That's also why the statue of Saint Lazarus is covered with sores. I never went to any of those processions, because I already told you that we were from Pinar del Rio and because in my house we were devotees of Cachita, Our Lady of El Cobre, who I know was the one who saved me and my children. But there's more. I admit I didn't know much about Saint Lazarus, but in Hialeah there's a church not far from here on the corner of 4th and 12th. He's a saint that belongs to a syncretic religion, or rather one that is worshipped by Blacks—or Afro-descendants as we say these days—even though here in Hialeah there aren't a lot of them."

Mercy took a break to get some water.

"Cubans built the church, even though it gets less publicity than the shrine. I have a friend who goes and sometimes I go with her. Basically all churches are the same because they all include the same God. Right? We go to mass on Sundays but yesterday there was a funeral mass because the little old man from the house on the corner died, right out front on the sidewalk. Look, I don't know what came over me, whether it was a vision or I fell asleep and was dreaming, but I felt a presence that told me I needed to pray for someone who was already dead, who'd been ill, and who couldn't rest in peace until Gladysita was back with us."

Maria didn't know what to think.

"So why did you ask me if I had gone to Tampa?"

"Because that's what they told me when I called your office."

Her answer reassured Maria and, although she never would believe in such things, she was more convinced than ever that the woman had some incomprehensible gift to see the future.

"And so what did you do?"

"I went straight to buy the statue of Saint Lazarus. Just yesterday my grandson helped me place it in the right spot. I would do anything to find my granddaughter. Don't think that I like it much; it even scares me a little, may God and Saint Lazarus forgive me, but I always follow what my dreams say. They've never led me astray."

"Have you said anything to your daughter?"

"No, no way…not to my grandson either. Not to anybody. Only you because nobody is going to believe me. Maybe not even you, but what do I know? Who knows, maybe something that I tell you might help you in the investigation."

"True, you never know…"

"I also don't want my daughter to get more nervous than she already is."

Maria was interested in knowing whether Gladys Elena had fessed up to her husband about the girl's paternity. She thought about stopping by to see if she was home, but she knew about mother's intuition and was afraid of giving it away, and that the woman would realize that she had found her daughter.

Even though Maria was sure that she had found her, until Alexis consented to the test and they had the results, it was best to keep quiet. For a moment she thought that maybe the grandmother knew more than she had told her, but she preferred not to push it. Mercy said goodbye with a kiss and a wink. When she raised her hand to wave goodbye, she announced: "We will see each other very soon, because it is almost Saint Lazarus Day, the 17th."

Maria looked at her watch. It was December 10th.

She was about to take the Palmetto Parkway when her cell rang. It was Smith. Alexis had agreed to take the DNA test.

Chapter 33

Days 40–42—Friday through Sunday, December 11 through 13, 2015

Maria couldn't meet with Keppler until Friday morning. She had already asked the Tampa police to send someone to take a saliva simple from Alexis Smith and to process the DNA as quickly as possible. But she wasn't sure that she had been effective in communicating the urgency of the case to them.

"Larry, maybe you can call and ask them to give it priority."

"Maria, if they have waited twenty-three years, what do a few more days matter?"

She didn't dare bring up Saint Lazarus or her own illusion that the families would spend Christmas together. She joked, "Now you're showing your gringo colors… Precisely because they have suffered for so long, they deserve to know the truth… Be more compassionate."

She knew that she could get away with those pokes at the boss as long as she did it in private and with a sweet tone.

"Ok, ok…get me in touch with the person you want me to talk to, and then later, take the rest of the week off."

"Larry, it's already Friday… I'll get caught up on the paperwork and see if we can close the case quickly and cleanly, and, if there aren't any emergencies, I'll be free this weekend, like always."

It was a privilege that she had earned through her years of service and her position as detective.

Maria began sifting through the file that was bulky by now. She remembered when she opened those two boxes, she saw the scarce information and the little baby seat they had pulled from the car that fell into the canal. She was replaying in her head her visits with Gladys Elena Lazo and her mother. She remembered the tip from Dr. John Erwin that the man could have been a murder victim. She rethought the moment she realized his identity was fake, how her friend Leo had guided her to the websites to figure out Alberto Raimundo Gonzalez Lazo's identity. And she thought about the enormous help that Don Joaquin del Roble had been. However, the case began to produce concrete clues after the visit to the writer Manuel Larrea in Miami Beach. That day she had a migraine, and she didn't feel like driving so far away, so she asked Fernandez to go with her. The young man had been a valuable assistant and a nice colleague, and even fun. Larrea was the first one to tell them about the couple who falsified documents and gave them the name and number of another writer, Jacinto Bengochea. She also remembered Rosa Blass in her elegant apartment in Surfside and the story of how her Jewish family had left Poland fleeing from poverty and how they had prospered in Cuba, just to lose everything all over again. Rosa was the one who had given them the information about the man they called *El Oso*. The interview with Bengochea in that café in Brooklyn had been decisive, above all when Fernandez persuaded him to go to the station and work with one of the artists to make a charcoal sketch of the counterfeiters' faces.

The calls that came in when the drawings were circulated had lead them, step by step, to locate the girl. The clues received from Odalys Fuentes, Altagracia Pena, and the little girl's teacher in Tampa accelerated things for them. The truth is that Fernandez's efforts of combing through the faces of soccer players at universities required time, stamina, and a lot of faith. And then, by human error, they went to the wrong address in Tampa. That was the darkest moment of the investigation. But now the reunion of mother and daughter was coming soon. She knew how much both families wanted it and feared it at the same time and, curiously, so did she. She had gotten emotionally involved in the case, in spite of how much that went against all the unwritten yet essential rules of her profession.

David had agreed to come by to pick her up at seven thirty for dinner. She left the office early to give herself extra time to go see her father. The old man received her as if he hadn't seen her in a month. Truth is, his hugs and smile were always a safe haven.

He poured her a beer without even asking. They talked about trivial things, like the weather, if Patrick was about to come home, and how they would celebrate the Christmas season. Her father didn't ask her about the case, but, as she was about to leave, he placed his large hands on each of her arms and looked her in the eye.

"Look, *mija*, you know what you're feeling. It's that adrenaline crash when we've been working a case for a long time, and it's about to end. I haven't wanted to ask you because I know there are confidential things that you shouldn't tell me, but I suspect that there are some loose ends to be tied up and that the case is practically solved and now you feel some type of void. But don't worry, new cases and life itself will fill it."

It never ceased to surprise her how well her father knew her. She kissed him goodbye and as she moved away, she teased:

"Good cops never lose their sense of smell. *Don* Patricio, I promise that I'll return soon with some news."

Maria realized that she was happily going to great trouble to get ready for David. There was a difference in wanting to look good for just any occasion as opposed to doing it to look good for a man. She really didn't know how to explain it, but it was different. Was she falling in love with David? She didn't want love complications in this phase of her life nor did she want to rack her brain figuring out emotions.

Apparently, David had also gone the extra mile so that it would be a special evening. He arrived with bouquet of flowers and an exquisite aroma of expensive cologne.

"I made reservations at Caffe Abbracci, if that sounds good to you… We can cancel them and go wherever you'd like."

"You know I love it…"

They dined at a secluded table and shared an appetizer and a bottle of good wine. She ordered risotto and he, lasagna. At dessert time, they couldn't decide between guava flan or creampuffs, so they settled on the cream and vanilla ice cream-filled pastries, topped with Grand Marnier and a bitter chocolate syrup.

"We can always eat guava flan at Versailles..." David argued.

They slowly relished that exquisite combination of flavors while looking into each other's eyes, as if anticipating the pleasures still awaiting them that night.

Over the weekend she paid bills, washed clothes, answered personal emails, looked at friends' Facebook pages, went to Publix to get groceries, and she even went to Miami International Mall to start some Christmas shopping.

But her subconscious betrayed her, and she couldn't stop thinking about the case. She visualized Soledad rescuing the baby from the car as it was about to fall into the water. She thought about the life of a woman always in fear of being found out and also about the other one who had not stopped searching for her daughter for more than two decades. As much as she always judged severely those who violated laws, Soledad's letter had left her with a strange impression, one that couldn't allow her to have a completely negative view of the woman. She thought that it was good they'd found the young woman when the mother who had raised her had already died and that there wouldn't be any prosecution and trial for kidnapping, which would have been devastating for Alexis.

Maria also thought about how she would find the right words to speak with mother and daughter. Without a doubt, she had never faced anything like this in her entire career. To think how indifferent she had been when she opened those boxes that Larry had left her in the conference room! Now she remembered how nervous her coworkers were that morning because nobody wanted to be stuck reopening an unresolved case. It had only been a month and a half, but to her it felt like she had lived with the subjects of this saga for a long time.

On Sunday, Patrick called her. Classes had ended two days ago but he had worked over the weekend. Starting the next day, he was free.

"Mami, do you mind if I go to New York for a few days first?"

"To New York?"

"Yes, but I promise that I'll be there for roast pork on Christmas Eve."

"Do you have money?"

"I can stretch it…"

"Are you driving alone?"

"No, I'm going with Mathilda to meet her family."

Her son never ceased to surprise her.

"Mami, don't worry, it isn't serious, it's not like we're going to get married tomorrow."

Maria laughed and surprised herself saying:

"If you want, invite her to come with you for Christmas, if her family doesn't mind."

Patrick became very happy, and she promised to send him some money to help with the trip.

"Don't worry, Mami. *Abuelo* already gave me some. Hang onto it for me for Christmas Eve."

"Have a good trip, *hijo*. Drive carefully…"

"You're the best mom in the world! *Ciao… ciaito…* Love you," he said with joy in his voice.

"Love you too…"

Chapter 34

Days 46–53—Thursday through Thursday, December 17 through 24, 2015

Maria had gotten up early and had gone to great lengths to get ready, as if indeed she were expecting Saint Lazarus to perform a miracle that day. She wasn't surprised when Dr. Erwin called her at ten o'clock that morning. He had just received the results from Alexis's DNA tests, and he was going to compare them to the ones he already had, the one he had finally extracted from the infant's hairbrush that the mother had saved and those of Alberto Gonzalez Lazo, Gladys Elena Lazo, and her husband Mauricio Lozano.

"If you head on over now, I'll be through by the time you get here, and you can take the report with you," the forensic doctor told her, knowing that she wouldn't proceed unless she had everything down in writing.

As soon as she got there, the doctor handed over the report. There wasn't any doubt about it. Alexis Smith was in fact Gladys Mercedes Lazo, and daughter of Gladys Elena and Mauricio and not the daughter of Raimundo Alberto Gonzalez Lazo.

The first thing she did was to call Alexis Smith's house. No one answered. She called her husband's cell phone, which he picked up on the third ring.

"I need to talk to your wife," she explained. "I have some news to give her."

"Can't you just tell me?"

"I'm sorry but…"

"Well, I'll leave a message for her to call you on her lunch break. She should be getting out of the classroom any minute now and should be free between twelve thirty and one o'clock."

Maria waited anxiously and, sure enough, one minute after twelve thirty the young woman returned her call.

She explained that she had been able to locate her real mother and other members of her family, and that her mother had never given up hope that she was alive and that she would be found one day, and that she had never stopped looking for her… She sensed that the young woman on the other end of the line had started to cry.

"When can I meet her?" Alexis's question took her by surprise.

"First, I need your permission to let her know that I've found you and then, if all agree, you can talk by phone and make arrangements."

"Right now I'm at school. Can you call back at four o'clock?"

"Sure, but do I have your permission to let your mother know that I've found you?"

"Of course, but just one question first… What's her name?"

"Gladys Elena."

"Gladys Elena…" Alexis repeated the name as if she were caressing it. "Tell her I'm sorry for everything that she has gone through…please."

"Look, Alexis, one last thing. Could you give your husband permission to send me Soledad's letter? No one's going to explain what happened better, and I'm sure if Gladys Elena reads it, she'll forgive her."

"I don't know…"

"Well, think about it… Right now I'm going to go see her and give her the good news. I'll have to do it cautiously so she doesn't faint."

Maria wasn't sure if she should call first or just stop by the house in Hialeah unannounced. She opted for the latter. She wasn't too surprised when Mercy appeared at the door with a smile from ear to ear.

"I've been expecting you," she said with a mischievous grin.

"Is your daughter home?"

Gladys Elena suddenly appeared. She was shaking like a leaf. Had Mercy told her to expect a miracle from Saint Lazarus or was it mother's intuition? Was it possible that she had lost her impenetrable detective face and that her expression showed that she was the bearer of good news?

Since all three of them were standing, it was Maria who spoke up first.

"Why don't we sit down, if that's ok?"

This time Gladys Elena showed her into the living room and not the little office as before.

Once there, Maria couldn't find any way to tell her other than just coming right out and bluntly telling her the news.

"We've found your daughter. She's fine. She doesn't live far away, in Tampa. She's married and you have a granddaughter. She's led a good life. The people who raised her have passed away. She's anxious to meet you."

The rest was just hugs, tears, and laughter.

When they calmed down a bit, Maria asked Gladys Elena:

"Have you spoken with your husband?"

"Yes, and he's going to be so happy, but…"—she glanced at her mother— "she's the one who doesn't know."

The grandmother smiled once again.

"Of course I know all about it. Nothing gets by me. The girl is Mauricio's daughter."

"Her name is now Alexis, Alexis Smith," Maria clarified. "I'm going to call her at four this afternoon, and I'll ask her to call you or for her permission to give you her number."

Both of them said goodbye to Maria with effusive gestures of gratitude and strong hugs.

"I told you Duchess. It's a miracle from Saint Lazarus!" the grandmother declared emphatically.

That very afternoon, Nicholas Smith sent Maria an email with the letter that Soledad had written to her daughter and permission to share it with her birth mother. Maria did so but not before speaking to her first and asking her not to judge the woman harshly.

Maria didn't know how the phone conversations went between Alexis and her mother, grandmother, and siblings, or if they even told her who her real father was. On December 22, as she was drinking her morning coffee at the same stand as she usually did, Maria received a call from Alexis. She was so nervous that Maria had to ask her to calm down just so she could understand her. She explained that she had thought about coming down by car but that her daughter gets carsick on long trips. Instead, she had a found a flight early on the twenty-fourth but hadn't been able to rent a car. Her family had told her not to worry about it, that they had offered to come pick her up at the airport, yet she was a bit nervous about it all.

"Detective Duquesne, I really hate to bother you, and I know it's Christmas Eve, but would there be any way you could possibly pick us up and take us to my family's house? I would feel so much better."

Maria gladly agreed and by eleven o'clock that morning, Alexis and Nicholas Smith along with their young daughter were sitting in her car with quite a few suitcases.

"As you can see, we're bringing a few gifts," Nicholas explained.

Maria started to speak to the young girl, but then realized she didn't know her name.

"Her name is Helen…"

"Her grandmother's going to be delighted that she has her middle name."

"I hadn't even realized that!"

"I forgot to ask you, Alexis, have you ever been to Miami?"

"Yes, a few months ago, we came for three days to see some close friends."

"Did you by chance go to a Heat game?"

"Why, yes, we did. How did you know? Wow, you can tell you're a detective…"

Maria just smiled.

The small house in Hialeah was decorated with balloons and welcome signs.

Maria got out with them but didn't want to go in.

"You go ahead, go on, it's a very private moment. They're a beautiful family. Everything's going to work out just fine," she said as she nudged them toward the front door that opened right away. She saw them go in, and, even from the yard, she could hear the uproar of laughter and excitement.

She put the car in drive and headed for home. Her father was waiting for her to put the pork shoulder in the oven and finish the final preparations for dinner. Patrick and Mathilda would be arriving any moment. Lourdes and Yolanda had said they'd also come by to drop off some gifts for their "adopted grandson." On Monday, she'd go back to work. She'd file a report with Keppler on how useful Fernandez had been. They'd assign her new cases.

Before leaving the Hialeah area, Maria saw more statues than ever before of Saint Lazarus covered with his purple cape. *I guess I never noticed before. Could he really be miraculous?* she asked herself. Suddenly, her eyes teared up, even though she wasn't quite sure why.

About the Author

Uva de Aragón (Havana, 1944) has published a dozen books of poetry, essays, short stories, novels, and one play. She comes from a family of Spanish and Cuban writers and continues to write mainly in Spanish, although she has resided in the United States since 1959. Some of her work, translated into English, has appeared in various anthologies. The bilingual edition of her award-winning novel *The Memory of Silence/ Memoria del silencio*, translated by Jeffrey C. Barnett (Cubanabooks, 2014) is being taught at several universities. For many years she was a columnist for *Diario Las Americas* and later *El Nuevo Herald*. Until her retirement in 2011, she was the associate director of the Cuban Research Institute at Florida International University. Dr. de Aragón graduated with a PhD in Latin American Literature from the University of Miami. She has received several literary awards in the United States and Europe. Thousands of readers around the world log into her blog *Habanera soy* uvadearagon.wordpress.com.

Mango Publishing, established in 2014, publishes an eclectic list of books by diverse authors—both new and established voices—on topics ranging from business, personal growth, women's empowerment, LGBTQ studies, health, and spirituality to history, popular culture, time management, decluttering, lifestyle, mental wellness, aging, and sustainable living. We were recently named 2019's #1 fastest growing independent publisher by *Publishers Weekly*. Our success is driven by our main goal, which is to publish high quality books that will entertain readers as well as make a positive difference in their lives.

Our readers are our most important resource; we value your input, suggestions, and ideas. We'd love to hear from you—after all, we are publishing books for you!

Please stay in touch with us and follow us at:
Facebook: Mango Publishing
Twitter: @MangoPublishing
Instagram: @MangoPublishing

LinkedIn: Mango Publishing
Pinterest: Mango Publishing

Sign up for our newsletter at www.mango.bz and receive a free book!

Join us on Mango's journey to reinvent publishing, one book at a time.

CPSIA information can be obtained
at www.ICGtesting.com
Printed in the USA
BVHW031034071019
560338BV00002B/1/P

9 781642 501247